THE DEBUTANTE'S SECOND CHANCE

KENTUCKY DEBUTANTES OF THE GILDED AGE
BOOK THREE

LISA M. PRYSOCK

CHAPTER ONE

The human body is the chariot; the self, the man who drives it; thought is the reins, and feelings, the horses.
—Plato

FEBRUARY 14, 1908
VELVET BROOKS FARM, LEXINGTON, KENTUCKY

"Is that you, Gladdie? It's Henry Billings...from the Lexington Stockyard." The clerk's voice crackled through the recently installed telephone line. "I've got a horse here for you, just arrived this morning with your name as the recipient."

"A horse? Are you certain, Henry? We weren't expecting any deliveries today, and certainly not a horse." Seated at Pa's desk in the library at their horse farm, Velvet Brooks, holding the receiver to her ear, Gladys Lyndon leaned forward. Surely, Henry was mistaken. Pa hadn't mentioned anything about a horse being shipped by train.

"Yes, I'm sure. She just arrived on the nine o'clock from New York. She's a real beauty too. Three years old, according to the paperwork."

"A filly? From New York?" Her brows rose. Pa wouldn't have forgotten to mention such an important detail, would he? He had been somewhat forgetful prior to his departure for South Carolina, a symptom of the strain he'd been under lately that had led to his recent stroke. But to forget a new horse purchase seemed unlikely even then. Or had he planned it as a Valentine's Day surprise?

"Probably another champion for your stables. When can you pick her up?" Henry sounded anxious, talking a bit fast. A variety of indistinguishable noise and voices in the background added confusion to the crackling on the line.

"*When* can we pick her up?" Gladdie repeated into the mouthpiece. Taking the base of the telephone with her, she swirled around in Pa's desk chair until facing the front of the house, the old floorboards creaking as she rose and stepped before one of the two windows. She parted the lace hanging between the drapes with one finger while holding the receiver to her ear, peering toward the big horse barn. It looked quiet outside, but the men employed by her father would be working hard inside the barn or doing something useful some-where on the property. And it was beginning to rain. She bit her lower lip. Maybe Hank Parker, the farm's manager, knew something about this horse. "It's so unexpected, Henry. I'll do my best to send someone over before the end of today, or I'll come myself."

"Very good. The sooner, the better." He cleared his throat. "Word of caution. She's on the feisty side. You may want to send a couple of farmhands or bring someone to help you."

Feisty? No wonder Henry sounded nervous. He'd probably had a tangle with the filly while unloading her from the train.

"Thanks for the warning. Someone will be there as soon as we can manage it. Does your paperwork indi-cate who the sender of this horse is?" Gladdie arched her brow and held her breath.

"Uh, let me check."

Rustling papers and more crackling on the line filled her ears.

"Ah. Here's what I'm looking for. There's some history about this horse amongst the papers the sender included." He paused and more papers shuffled. "No, it just says a gift for Miss Gladys Lyndon. Unfortunately, the filly was sent anonymously, so I can't help any with who the sender is, but if I knew, I'd tell you."

"A gift for me? Hmm." She had a couple of ideas who might be behind such a grand gesture, but both possibilities seemed unlikely.

"Yes, Gladdie. I'm curious to know who sent her too. On another note, how's your pa doing?"

"Mama says he improves a little each day. Thank you for asking, Henry." Gladdie untwined the long cord wrapped around her hand and turned around to face the desk again. She set the slim base of the telephone back onto Pa's desk, delighted with the convenience. Her father had dragged his feet for years about installing a telephone, just as he did about automobiles, but it was long past time Velvet Brooks entered the world of progress. What a surprise it had been the day the telephone installers had arrived.

Speaking of surprise...Pa and Mama would be shocked to see the jodhpurs she currently wore with her riding boots.

"Yes, of course. He's in our prayers. I guess we'll see you soon, then. Remember now, we close at five o'clock. Happy Valentine's Day to y'all."

"Thank you." She leaned forward to speak into the funnel-shaped mouthpiece. "Happy Valentine's Day to y'all at the stockyards as well. Goodbye for now." Because of her preoccupation with fitting in with her elite friends of New York society, Mama would cringe to hear Gladdie using words in her Southern drawl with no regard for proper grammar, but even her mother displayed her Kentucky heritage now and then.

Gladdie disconnected the call by hanging the receiver on the device, frowning. Would Pa have shipped her a horse on his way through New York before heading south to Chesapeake Manor? He had traveled with Mama, Gladdie's sister Veronica, her sister's husband, Edward, and their two sons—her nephews, Edward Junior and Creighton—to Edward's boyhood vacation home situated on the coast of South Carolina. They'd arrived ten days ago, hoping to improve Creighton's constantly delicate health with the salty ocean air and give Pa the rest he needed so much to recover.

It seemed highly unlikely that her father would have had time to purchase a horse while traveling through New York by train—if indeed they had even stopped in the state. Perhaps Pa had ordered the horse *before* his departure, or maybe this had something to do with her sister's husband's family who lived in New York. And yet...Mama had failed to mention any new horse in her first letter, nor had she mentioned the filly in any of their few telephone conversations.

The ticking of the clock above the fireplace mantel caused her to glance up. Almost noon-thirty. Pa would be finishing his luncheon, maybe even taking a leisurely afternoon lie-down by now. Rather than disturb his rest or a meal, she'd telephone later and ask if he knew anything about this turn of events.

If not Pa, had Harvey sent the filly? Harvey Higginbottom, a writer for the *Lexington Gazette*, was the gentleman her parents and Grandfather Lyndon considered a suitable candidate to become her future husband, but someone she didn't find herself attracted to romantically. What did they admire in Harvey that she failed to see?

Sure, he owned a comfortable two-story house with a big front porch in town. He had an interesting career as a newspaper journalist. He attended her church, too, but he was a quirky sort of fellow with an overly meticulous nature.

Shaking her head, she crossed her arms over her chest. No, not even the gift of a champion filly could entice her into becoming Mrs. Harvey Higginbottom. If he had sent such an extravagant present, she should return it at once—except for the fact she didn't know if he had sent the horse. Nor could she bring herself to call him to ask. It would be considered forward of her to telephone him—except perhaps to thank him for sending the gift.

She drummed her fingers on Pa's desk. Harvey might be the most likely sender, since he *had* recently returned from New York on some sort of journalism assignment. He resided next door to her grandfather, Colonel Lyndon, who'd served in the war between the North and the South on Lincoln's side. Her grandfather had established the legacy of Velvet Brooks before retiring to live in the city where things were easier for him and her grandmother. Harvey loved chatting about old war stories and politics with Grandfather Lyndon. They relished long discussions about horses and farms since Harvey had grown up at Fern Ridge, a small horse farm in the vicinity of Velvet Brooks.

Hadn't he mentioned something about a surprise the last time he'd called on her? She rose from Pa's leather chair. Circling around to the front of the desk, she paced, hands clasped behind her back as she tried to recall. Yes. She'd offered him tea in the sitting room to be polite. But a *horse*? It seemed rather presumptuous, even for Harvey.

Nonetheless, despite the fact he sometimes worked from his city home when he wasn't at his *Gazette* office, she simply refused to telephone him to inquire about the matter. Why get his hopes up for a match between the two of them with a call? While she considered him a friend, Harvey Higginbottom was merely another nice gentleman she would never marry.

She had no intention of marrying anyone.

Just as her oldest sister, Veronica, had nursed a hidden broken heart before meeting Edward, Gladdie's heart ached, and she remained firmly convinced it would never fully mend. After Clay Grinstead had jilted her, failing to show up to catch the train to Richmond, Kentucky, for their elopement, she'd telephoned her grandfather, a man who had a little faith in modern inventions, the next morning. "Grandpa, I'm in trouble. Big trouble. Will you come and get me?"

She'd rushed into Pa's and Mama's embrace the moment her grandfather brought her inside the front door. She could still remember, after telling the whole story, what her mother had said. "Well, honey, we don't know why things happen the way they do. Sometimes they don't make sense until years later. We must do the best we can to go on in the meantime. Find purpose and meaning in life in other ways, through whatever God gives your hands to do."

Gladdie had eventually heard the rumors that her beau had betrayed her, marrying Alice Parker within a few days or perhaps hours of when he should have shown up on the train to elope with Gladdie. The only saving grace had been the fact it was a secret elopement. If he'd jilted her in front of all of Lexington, she'd never have survived.

Sure, folks had gossiped plenty about the fact Clay had married Alice when he'd been courting Gladdie unofficially. An ache still pulsed with every beat of her heart, but no one seemed to think it would still be so. Nothing could be further from the truth, even after all these years. She had turned twenty-three a few months ago, and by now, he would be about twenty-six. Seven years had gone by.

Her parents and most other family members now urged her to consider marrying Harvey...or Percy Sullivan...or some other gentleman caller. She preferred to make a game of hiding from the callers with a bevy of excuses, despite Mama's protests.

After all, they had more important matters to contend with than marrying her off—chiefly, Pa's failing health due to his stroke and the survival of Velvet Brooks. The stroke had left Pa with problems not only with his memory, but also in his speech and mobility.

According to the doctor, he needed rest and tranquility to recover. Hence, his journey to Chesapeake Manor on the South Carolina coast to enjoy Edward's family vacation home.

Things had changed at the estate where Gladdie had spent her whole life. While the Sullivans still owned the horse farm on most of their western border below Rose Glen Cottage, the owners of Blue Acres on their eastern perimeter had sold their farm and moved away to live in another state. Someone had torn down their old farmhouse and currently, what looked to be a mansion was under construction. Everyone stared at the limestone mansion as they passed Blue Acres, curious about who the owner might be.

For another thing, her sisters weren't as involved with Velvet Brooks as they might have preferred before they married—and at a time Gladdie needed them most. Her older sister, Delia Williams, had her hands full caring for her toddler, Isadora, and her husband Jake's three nieces. Not to mention the country inn and boardinghouse they operated in their home across the street and a second baby on the way. Jake had a few horses they occasionally entered into races too.

Her oldest sister, Veronica, and her husband, Edward Beckett, still resided for most of each year on ten acres of neighboring land at Rose Glen Cottage, a wedding gift from Pa. But as proud owners of their own business in Lexington, they focused on making Edward's artwork a success. Beckett's Art Gallery kept them quite busy—when they weren't galivanting off to New York or South Carolina. Unfortunately, their second son, Creighton, did not enjoy the same good health as his older brother, Eddie Junior. Veronica spent most of her time providing extra care for Creighton, who'd been susceptible to colds and fevers ever since his birth.

And now any issues at the farm fell to Gladdie. She carried a heavy load, and only the Lord could see them through. Big changes in the horseracing industry weighed heavily on everyone's minds. Worry was evident in the eyes of their staff. With so many racecourses closing around the country because of new laws enacted due to bookmakers skimming the purse—not to mention a growing sentiment against betting and horseracing in general—fewer folks contacted them to train their horses. And with fewer races, chances of winning a purse had become even more elusive, making the sport less lucrative for breeders and trainers.

The ledger book lay open on her father's desk where she entered income in one column and expenses in the accounts payable column. Some funds remained in their account at the bank, but the figure decreased with each passing day. If the Phoenix Stakes Race at the Lexington Association Track and the Derby at Churchill Downs went on as usual, and if they could take any of the top winning places, she could use the funds to make payroll and keep Velvet Brooks afloat without dipping into Pa's savings.

Her hands flew to her hips. She really should stop pacing and also stop her thoughts from becoming a jambalaya soup. She'd best head to the barn and ask if Hank could designate two strong men to wrangle Miss Feisty Filly into the horse wagon. And sooner rather than later so Henry wouldn't have a conniption at the stockyards.

A tingle of anticipation shot through Gladdie. It had been a long while since they'd won any races. What if this filly turned out to be a champion just as Henry had said? Could the new horse help her save Velvet Brooks in Pa's absence?

CHAPTER TWO

Pleasant words are as a honeycomb, sweet to the soul,
and health to the bones.
- Proverbs 16:24, KJV

Standing outside on the columned veranda at Velvet Brooks, Gladdie waited to greet the farm manager, Hank Parker, and their hand, Nathaniel Hartley, as they arrived in the horse wagon with their mystery guest from the stockyard. She couldn't consider the horse anything other than a guest until she knew who'd sent her and why.

The rain had stopped, and she took in the merits of the chestnut-colored horse from a safe distance as the filly neighed and stomped while the men cautiously steered her out of the wagon. Possessing long legs and intelligent eyes, she displayed feisty mannerisms in her eagerness to step out of the confining space.

Gladdie had spoken to her mother, Eleanor Lyndon, shortly before the men had arrived. Mama, in a muffled voice, had asked Pa about the filly while Gladdie waited on the line. But she'd come back to the telephone with as much curiosity as everyone else at Velvet Brooks. "We don't have any idea who sent the horse, Gladdie. Let us know if you find out."

"Certainly, Mama." She'd hung up the phone with furrowed brows. Surely, time would tell. In the meantime, they'd simply have to search for clues.

Carter attempted to pat the filly's nose as he kept a firm hold on the lead to her bit and bridle. He led the horse to stand alongside the edge of the veranda where Gladdie could inspect her. Would the filly stop sashaying those elegant yet sturdy hooves and permit their groom to make a connection with her?

The horse bristled and shook her chestnut mane, then shifted her weight and flicked her long reddish-brown tail as the groom reached out in a second attempt to pat her. Her ears perked up as he spoke softly, and for a moment, she allowed Carter the courtesy of wooing her.

"Atta girl." The groom smiled gingerly as she began to settle. "You're gonna love it here, Feisty Filly."

"Miss Cantankerous will need a name." Hank winked at Gladdie. Then, with curiosity in his eyes, he came to stand behind Carter, crossing his arms as he surveyed the horse with as much wariness as the equine offered him. No relation to former Senator Parker—Alice Parker's father—Hank had also been no help concerning the filly's origins when Gladdie approached him in the barn about picking her up at the stockyard.

Gladdie remained on the veranda, giving the horse a chance to adapt to new surroundings before introducing herself. Yet the men would hope to head to their cabins on the back forty soon to begin getting ready for tonight's Valentine's Dance hosted in the Phoenix Hotel's grand ballroom. She glanced at the timepiece pinned to the tweed riding jacket that paired so nicely with her jodhpurs. About ten minutes before quitting time.

Carter would be escorting his wife, Grace, their faithful lady's maid and all-around household staff member, to the dance. Hank would take his wife, Willamena, their cook. Most likely, their extra farmhand, Nathan, also had a date, just as Red Brickman, their trainer, probably did. Delia and Jake would be getting ready about now too.

The only person besides herself who wouldn't be attending the dance was their butler, Martin Everly. Martin would bring a tea tray to Gladdie in the library. And there she would pass a quiet and comfortable evening. Mama had pressed her in her last letter about attending the dance, but why do so if one didn't intend to get to know any of one's dance partners?

Nathaniel's voice disrupted her thoughts. "Miss

Cantankerous or Feisty Filly would be good names for her. She kicked at the wagon walls and neighed in protest most of the way here." Nathan stood even with Hank beyond Carter, maintaining his distance with a wary eye too. "Or maybe you could call her Miss Unpredictability."

Gladdie chuckled softly. "A nice name idea. I'll add it to the list of possibilities."

He smiled, tipping his hat in her direction, then returning his gaze to the horse—no doubt in case she tried anything on the wild side. "Going to the dance with one of your many admirers tonight, Miss Gladdie?"

She shook her head. "Not me, Nathan. I've got a date with one of my embroidery projects and a good book. I hope y'all can get this lady settled into one of our stalls for the evening and that you each have a fine time at the dance."

"Thank you, Miss Gladdie," Carter said on behalf of the men.

Ready to introduce herself to their four-legged guest, she stepped forward beside Carter and faced the horse. "Welcome to Velvet Brooks, mystery darling."

When the filly allowed her to stroke her nose a few times, Gladdie smiled. She wasn't imagining the softening in the horse's eyes. Did she approve of Gladdie's soft voice and gentle touch?

She reached inside the pocket of her jodhpurs and offered an outstretched palm with a few apple wedges, stolen from the kitchen right under Willamena's nose, causing the cook to shake her head and shoo her away. The woman had smiled, though. She hadn't seemed to have minded Gladdie borrowing from the apple pie which would become that evening's dessert. Indeed, Willamena was well accustomed to such antics, especially when the slices were for a new horse. The filly gobbled them up in seconds, earning chuckles from the fellas when she nudged Gladdie, searching and sniffing for more treats.

Gladdie joined the crew in laughter, unable to suppress her giggling as the horse nudged her again and sniffed the length of her arm to her hand. "I guess she really loves apples. We haven't had a horse nudge us that way in a long time."

Reaching in her pocket one more time, she produced the last two wedges. The horse scarfed them down and then bobbed her head a few times before nudging Gladdie again, an indication of not only her love for apples, but a sign that friendship could be achieved with this equine.

Gladdie glanced over her shoulder at the men with a wide smile. "Such a personality! Yes, I think she'll fit right in here."

Hank stepped closer and handed her some folded paperwork from his back pocket.

She glanced at the papers and tucked them under one arm. "Thank you, Hank. I'll give some thought to a name after I read up on her history, and when we've had a chance to get to know her. Then I'll pass this along to Red for our files."

"I'm sure he'd like to see how she does on the track." Hank uncrossed his arms.

"Me too. As soon as possible. Thanks for picking her up, boys. I only wish we knew who sent her to us. Don't get too attached. We may have to return her to the sender...if we ever learn who that is."

Hank scratched behind his ear. "That is a quandary, for sure, but we'll get her settled in for the night. Tomorrow, Red can plan a training agenda for her. When she's ready for the track, we'll come and get you. I can't wait to see how she does too."

"Perfect." Gladdie patted the filly's nose one last time. Then she stepped out of the way, pausing on the veranda to admire the newcomer while the three men led their new equine friend toward the barn. What else could she do for now but embrace the magnificent animal as if she were any other potential champion Pa brought to Velvet Brooks?

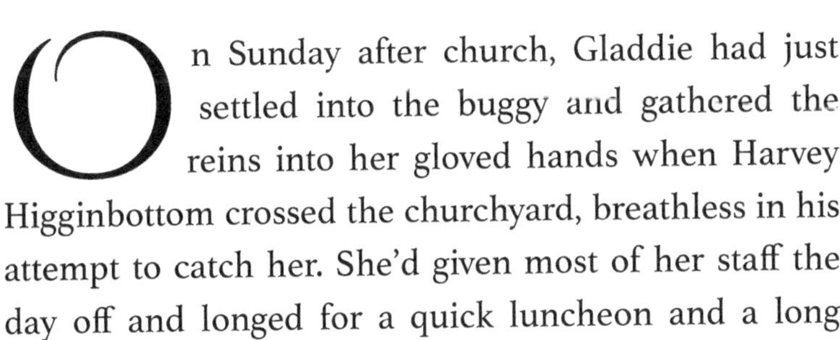

On Sunday after church, Gladdie had just settled into the buggy and gathered the reins into her gloved hands when Harvey Higginbottom crossed the churchyard, breathless in his attempt to catch her. She'd given most of her staff the day off and longed for a quick luncheon and a long

Sunday afternoon nap. Ugh. She'd almost made her escape. But now would be the perfect occasion to ask about the new horse. She might have done so before church, except she'd arrived with barely enough time to slip into her pew before the service began.

Leaning forward, she offered a warm smile. "Hello, Harvey. A fine sermon on the merits of being a good steward. Wouldn't you agree?"

He placed a hand on the side of her buggy and nodded, returning the smile, pushing his spectacles farther up on his nose. "Indeed. Are you having lunch with your grandparents this afternoon, Gladdie? They've invited me to dine with them since I've just returned from New York. Might we have the pleasure of your company too?"

The wind blew her veil away from her face, but she pulled it back down to hide her discomfort at his question. "No, I'm sorry to say I won't be dining with them this afternoon, though they did invite me. My sister Delia and her husband will be there with their four children, though. It so happens, I've plum worn myself out at Velvet Brooks this week with Pa away in South Carolina. I've been painting the fencing when we have nice weather."

Disappointment registered in his expression. His chest drew up before he released a long sigh. "Oh, well, perhaps another time, then?"

"Of course. Speaking of being a good steward, I did want to thank you for the surprise I'm guessing you sent on Valentine's Day." She mustered another smile, hoping it wasn't too flirtatious as she tilted her head. But the puzzled look spreading across his face told her he had no idea what she was talking about. Gladdie's smile faded as her confusion mounted. "You did mention a surprise the last time I saw you. I figured you must be the one who sent the filly."

"A filly?" His brows furrowed, and his blank look dissolved into disappointment as he blinked his blue eyes behind the round metal frames of his spectacles. "I do wish I could claim to have sent you a filly on Valentine's Day. What a fine idea from someone smarter than myself, but sadly, it wasn't me. No, I planned to bring you some starters from the lilacs on either side of my front porch, since you enjoy them so much."

Her mouth dropped open. "It wasn't you who sent the filly?" If Harvey hadn't sent her, and Pa hadn't ordered the filly, then who on earth had shipped the horse all the way from New York?

"No, I'm sorry, it wasn't me." Harvey shrugged while loosening his tie. "And I do hope you aren't working too terribly hard."

"Oh." She sighed. Too bad the mystery would remain a mystery for a while longer. No need to respond about working too hard. She had little choice in the matter, so she stiffened her back, perking up a bit. "Well, I do love the idea of those lilac starters. Just drop them off whenever it suits you. I guess I should be on my way. I'm going straight to bed for a long afternoon rest." In addition to fence-painting, she'd spent far too many hours looking over the books for the farm and worrying about spring planting being on time. She couldn't remember when she'd worked so hard.

"Thank you, Miss Gladdie. Maybe I'll see you later this week or next." He tipped his bowler hat and bowed, stepping aside so she could exit the churchyard.

"Goodbye for now." She snapped the reins gently, urging her horse forward.

Gladdie bit her lip as the buggy rolled along at a steady pace past greening hills, four-board fences, and low stone walls, the sun not quite warm enough to break the last of winter's chill. Who could have sent the horse? Not knowing was so vexing. Maybe Percy Sullivan? He had enough wealth to send such a gift, but it seemed unlikely since he hadn't called on her in at least six months after pursuing her on and off for several years. She'd assumed he'd finally given up on the idea of her succumbing to his wishes for an engagement. And wouldn't he have called on her by now if he'd sent the horse?

Other than Percy, she could only think of Edward's father, Leviticus Beckett, or Aunt Mae, both of whom lived in New York. Perhaps she'd contact them to ask, but she wasn't close with either of them. Veronica and Delia had spent some weeks in New York with Aunt Mae, but Gladdie had never gotten to know her that well, even on her aunt's trips to Kentucky—rare due to Aunt Mae's disapproval of horseracing.

With the mystery behind the horse unsolved, how could she even name the filly? Maybe she could at least grant the horse a stable name for now. Perhaps Lady M, short for Lady Mystery.

Accepting expensive gifts raised all sorts of questions and concerns. What if the sender expected something she couldn't give in return?

CHAPTER THREE

Unexpressed emotions will never die. They are buried alive and will surface later in an uglier form.
—Sigmund Freud

MARCH 2, 1908
LEXINGTON, KENTUCKY

Gladdie turned onto Main Street in Pa's wagon two weeks later to shop for supplies for Velvet Brooks. Where had all of the traffic come from, and why were so many folks milling about in front of the shops and businesses? A bottleneck ahead of where she needed to park blocked her view, but at least she was able to pull the wagon close to the grocer's shop.

Purchasing goods made her stomach twist in knots

since she'd be depleting more funds from Pa's bank account to do so, but it couldn't be helped. Willamena had written down everything they needed, and nothing on the list could be avoided. Flour, sugar, tea, coffee, cornmeal, baking powder, and a few other items. Plus, a birthday gift for Mary, Jake's youngest niece. After all, Ruby, Ella, and Mary had become like daughters to Delia and Jake, and precious family members to all of the Lyndons.

As for the rest of the list, it might've been easier for Willamena to write down what they *weren't* out of at this point. They'd managed to get through the winter months with only a few trips to town for supplies, but as spring approached, they'd run low on most everything.

How did Mama manage it each year? Even the preserves she'd canned before winter were beginning to look scant on the shelves, partly because Gladdie had delivered so many jars of jam and jelly—most of it made from the abundant supply of fruit grown at Velvet Brooks—to the local orphanage, among other pantry items. It was her way of keeping her dream alive of having a school for orphans someday. And she would not be sorry for giving.

After she tethered the team to a hitching post, familiar male voices speaking exuberantly from the middle of Main Street drew her attention as she stepped onto the boardwalk.

Tightening the elegant scarf over her large hat as a

gust of wind threatened to dislodge it, she turned to face the street, and her mouth fell open.

Clay?

Clay Grinstead had returned to Lexington? No, it couldn't possibly be true.

She blinked and tried to close her mouth, but it only dropped open again. When had he arrived? She hadn't seen him at church, but then he hadn't attended her church except as her guest a few times. No, he had attended the local Presbyterian church with his family… and Alice Parker's.

Both mounted on fine steeds, Clay and Thaddeus Sullivan hunched low, seemingly waiting for the traffic to clear. Were they about to race?

Would a sheriff put a stop to this? No officers around presently. Even if miscreants were caught, the courts would only impose a three-dollar fine. According to Grandfather Lyndon and Grandfather Spencer, racing horses on the streets of Lexington went way back in history. The townsfolk were proud of their street racing legacy. Few would try to stop it.

Gladdie usually agreed with the sentiment, but today, the race irked her.

Thaddeus was the most irresponsible of the Sullivan clan. His pa, Harold Sullivan, stood across the street in front of Sullivan's Savings & Loan, wearing a fashionable black suit and rocking on his feet with pride as he observed the start of the race. Harold also owned a fine hotel in Richmond, not to mention one of the finest horse farms in Kentucky adjoining Velvet Brooks. Naturally, Harold would pay the fine if Thaddeus couldn't, and that would be the end of it.

Thaddeus would never grow up, or so it seemed, not even when he'd finally married someone else after Delia chose Jake over him. Thaddeus had settled on Miss Edna Tremont, a plain and homely sort who was known for singing off-key at many a social function. Unfortunately, with his reputation in tatters after Jake had confronted him about his underhanded deeds—sabotaging races and Jake's business—before the best of Lexington and Kentucky society, not even his father's money had been able to secure him a more refined bride. Seeing Clay with him now caused her eyes to widen. They'd never been the best of friends.

And why did Clay have the audacity to look so handsome upon his stallion? Was she in some sort of bad dream? Couldn't he return to wherever he'd come from?

Julius Anderson, a close friend of Thaddeus, stood across the street, holding up a white handkerchief. It fluttered in the chilly March breeze while dangling from his hand. Julius hollered, ""On your mark. Get ready." Then he waved the scrap of fabric with a downward, sweeping motion. "Yaw!"

Clay and Thaddeus took off, galloping down Main Street, their horses thundering past Gladdie and a great many other curious onlookers. Had Julius meant to throw Clay off by not using the word "go"? It hadn't ruined Clay's fine start, but it wouldn't surprise her if Julius had attempted to give Thaddeus an edge.

Would a conveyance—perhaps one of those noisy modern automobiles—come barreling through an intersection and run into one of their beautiful horses? Gladdie resisted the urge to close her eyes as the horses galloped onward.

Squinting, she spotted Arthur Breckenridge and what appeared to be his younger brother, Todd, standing on the corners of the next two intersections to ward off any traffic as the horses barreled down the road. At least they had posted lookouts, but it seemed the Breckenridge boys would never outgrow their antics, not even as men in their thirties.

The riders thundered toward a man at the third intersection who appeared to be Gebhart Pickett. He pulled a scarf taut above his head, representing the finish line.

If Delia could see this display, she would shake her head and might even drag Gladdie away, but for some reason, Gladdie couldn't resist watching the outcome of the race. Only, she dared not let Clay find her here. She wasn't ready to speak to Clay now...if ever.

"What are they racing for?" A lady standing nearby gawked after Clay and Thaddeus.

An excellent question. What *were* they racing for? Gladdie remained silent, concealing her eagerness to discover the answer.

Miss Daphne Broadhurst, an assistant librarian at

the library where Delia used to volunteer, sidled up. "Clay Grinstead wants an invitation to the Annual Sullivan Spring Ball. I heard Thaddeus say if Clay could beat his horse in a straight, flat heat through town, he'd secure an invitation for him from his mother. I'm not sure why Clay would want an invitation to the ball, though, since my neighbor said his wife passed away not that long ago. I'd think he'd still be in mourning."

Alice had passed away recently? Was it true? Had he returned to sink roots here?

Gladdie took solace in the fact none of the women mentioned her former whirlwind romance with Clay. Perhaps they didn't know about it, didn't remember, or maybe they were too polite to say anything.

"What if it's a dead heat?" the first lady inquired. "Looks like an awful close race to me."

"In the event of a tie, they'll go again. Thaddeus said so before the race." Miss Broadhurst kept a firm hold on the brim of her hat as another chilly breeze swept over them.

Another lady placed her hands on her hips. "Sounds to me as if Clay is in the market for a new wife. A fine catch he'll make too. I heard he inherited all of his wife's money and bought a nice farm somewhere in the area. But what does Thaddeus win if Clay loses?"

Gladdie clamped her mouth shut instead of releasing a gasp. Of course, Clay *would* have money on top of his good looks. The Parkers he'd married into had been wealthy. If they'd all passed on and left their estate and all of their holdings to Clay, he'd be enormously rich.

Clay's horse shot forward as they approached the third intersection.

A lady she hadn't met before peered down the street. "I'd like to know what Thaddeus wins if Clay loses, too, but it doesn't appear as if that Sullivan boy will win this time. Look at Grinstead's horse go!"

"I think Thaddeus has his eye on Clay's fine saddle," someone else said.

Gladdie didn't turn to look for the owner of the voice because Clay's horse crossed the finish line ahead of Thaddeus's horse by two or three nose lengths. Not a furlong by any means, but several nose lengths were considered an indisputable victory for her former beau. Vigorous cheers and clapping erupted along both sides of the street.

Oh, dear Lord, what are You doing to my heart? Why has this man come back to Lexington?

"My guess is, Thaddeus Sullivan enjoys the thrill of the race more than any prize." Miss Broadhurst nodded toward the two gentlemen astride their horses.

Simmering beneath her hat, Gladdie chided herself. She shouldn't have negative thoughts about her former beau. Why did she find it hard to be happy for him after all of these years?

Clay had grown up a coal miner's son, and the Parkers had owned mines in numerous locations outside of Kentucky. Since Gladdie had attended the

Lexington Finishing School for Ladies with Alice, it made the betrayal sting all the more. Alice was supposed to have been her friend. Had Alice's family wealth been an incentive for Clay to marry her?

After the wedding, in quick succession, the Grinstead and Parker families had moved away. Not long after, Alice's grandfather, Judge Parker, had retired from public life. He and his wife sold their Lexington home and left the area. When Alice's father, Senator Parker, finished his term, he left Kentucky too. Rumors swirled about where they'd all gone, but Gladdie had been too wounded to separate truth from fiction.

The memories flashed before her mind's eye as Thaddeus congratulated Clay with a pat on the back from astride his horse. Couldn't Thaddeus be a little less sportsmanlike today?

Why did the good Lord allow some undeserving folks like Clay to succeed in so many areas of life, while others, perhaps more deserving, seemed to struggle so much? Then again, she shouldn't question the God she served. He only allowed suffering to mold character into people or for some other good reason. Maybe affliction and suffering were what made the great truly capable of amazing things.

Biting her lower lip as Clay and Thaddeus trotted toward the starting line, she had to admit the affliction of losing Clay had given her humility and shaped her into a godly woman. It had driven her to prayer, a life of devotion in reading the Scriptures, and doing her best to serve the Lord. Would she ever have a chance of doing something remarkable for the Lord?

But why didn't she feel any happiness for her former beau's success? Why couldn't she at least empathize with the harsh reality of him having become a widower at a young age? Did she detect the lingering sting and pangs of bitterness, sorrow, unforgiveness, and resentment in her heart?

She'd need a good week of sulking to come to terms with this turn of events, but Gladdie couldn't stand another minute of listening to the women surrounding her. Not to mention, Clay was headed in her direction atop his glorious stallion. Horseracing might run in her blood far more than the blood of the city spectators, but not one bone in her body could cheer for the victor, much less congratulate him. She had to find a way of escape before Clay saw her, but she found herself mesmerized as folks crowded around him to reach up with a handshake or pat his horse as he passed by.

Hands on her hips, she could barely refrain from fuming as he and Thaddeus rode their mounts toward the starting line through the sea of folks. It would take some time to get over his arrival...and how handsome he looked...so she could squash the indignation and anger welling up on the inside. But even then, she could never consider this man an old friend as Thaddeus apparently did. Clay Grinstead could not be trusted. She'd barely survived the emotional chaos from his actions.

Gladdie spun to head inside the store, but the crowd made it impossible to escape.

"If you'll excuse me...excuse me, please..." She attempted to thrust a shoulder sideways into the crowd, turning and twisting to weave her way forward, but the crowd behind her had grown, and people had no room to let her pass.

She'd barely managed to squeeze past two strangers to step a few feet closer to the store entrance when Clay's familiar voice rang out.

"Gladdie? Miss Gladdie Lyndon? Is that you?"

Drat! Too late. How had he recognized her? She wasn't even facing the street. At least she'd worn her best walking suit and one of her finest hats if she must acknowledge him. Or could she keep going and pretend she hadn't heard him?

"See you later, Gladdie," Daphne called out.

Drat again! Gladdie's eyes squeezed shut as dread gripped her heart.

She turned to wave at Daphne with a weak smile before facing Clay. He had dismounted and now headed straight for her, a lead still in his hand. Could she dive toward the ground and crawl under folks to make a grand escape? Fling herself into the crowd and pray they parted for her to pass through? Push her way through as if she were a bull?

"Ah, Gladdie. It *is* you!" His voice floated over a few more folks passing between them, but he tethered his horse and stepped up to her in a matter of seconds. "How good it is to see you again."

Goodness, his shoulders were much broader than they'd been when he was nineteen. But she couldn't let his good looks deter her from conveying the fact that she had no intention of allowing him any place in her life.

He offered a warm smile, his blue eyes dancing as he removed his hat from his blond wavy hair, something akin to shyness at their awkward encounter flashing in his expression. He recovered quickly, standing up taller. "You haven't changed a bit. Just as beautiful as the first day I laid eyes on you, Gladdie Lyndon. How've you been?"

Was his shyness an indication of remorse for his actions? And rightly so!

Gladdie kept her eyes trained on him while she squared her shoulders and tilted her chin upward. "Well, if it isn't the very last person I'd prefer to see in my lifetime."

Pain flashed through his eyes. "That's no way to greet an old friend. C'mon, Gladdie. It's me, Clay. We grew up together." He offered another warm smile. "I know we have much to discuss about what happened..."

When had he grown so tall? She had to hold onto her hat when she looked up at him. "Nothing to discuss. I know everything I need to know about Clay Grinstead, a man who breaks his promises. A man whose word means nothing. A man who doesn't exist to me."

She turned on her heels to leave, but he caught hold of her arm. She grimaced and he let go.

"The things that happened were years ago, Gladdie. We were just kids. There were circumstances beyond my control. Can we let bygones be bygones? What say you permit me to escort you to the Sullivan Spring Ball, and we start anew? A second chance, if you will..."

Anger coursed so swiftly through her mind and veins that she didn't hear half of whatever he said. The man had caused her years of heartache and sorrow. "A second chance? You must be dreaming."

"Yes, maybe I am dreaming, but think of it, Gladdie. Wouldn't it be grand for us to be together? To begin again? I've thought about you for years... Can we have a cup of coffee at the bakery together? A chance for me to explain what happened?"

His brows rose with what she regarded as false hope while he turned those pleading sky-blue eyes on her, his hand reaching out to rest on her arm. How utterly ridiculous of him to try and charm his way back into her good graces with his gentle touch and flattery.

"Oh, no. We won't be having a cup of coffee at any bakery together. I choose not to remember us. And you are the very last person I'd ever consider dancing with. Or doing anything else. Goodbye, Clay." She jerked her arm away from him and hurried away, determined to flee before she burst into tears.

The crowd had finally thinned, and no one blocked her path inside the grocer's shop this time. She marched away with her head held high, but why did she tremble? Why were her hands balled into fists? Why did the loud clicking of her boot heels seem to echo in the store and straight through the emptiness in her chest?

She could hardly wait to return to the safety of Velvet Brooks, far from the ilk of Clay Grinstead! Why had he come back just when she'd finally gotten herself together?

CHAPTER FOUR

There are many wonderful places in the world, but one
of my favorite places is on the back of my horse.
—Rolf Kopfle, renowned horse trainer

MARCH 5, 1908
LOTTIE BELLE FARM, KENTUCKY

Clay straightened his tie, stretching his neck and
chin as he did so. Then he tugged on his vest,
making sure it was in place before knocking on the
door of Lottie Belle Country Inn & Boarding.

No answer. Maybe they hadn't heard his Ford Model
S Roadster when he'd pulled into the drive. A child's
giggle and footsteps stirring told him someone was at

home, as did the occasional splashing of water into troughs coming from the barn. He knocked again.

While he waited, he surveyed the farm across the street, Velvet Brooks, situated next door to the property he'd recently purchased from out of state through the help of an attorney. No sign of Gladdie, sadly, but he could see some of their beautiful horses grazing and some men tending various tasks around the horse barn. The house at the end of the long, tree-lined drive looked as inviting as he remembered it. Two stories. Whitewashed. Black shutters. Four narrow columns across the front. Sugar maples spread their branches, and the spring leaves offered a hearty welcome.

He'd soon see more of Gladdie once he convinced her sister to rent some rooms to him. Three rooms, to be precise. One for himself, another for Olympia and Emery, and one for his sister, Callie. The children waited in town at a boardinghouse under the care of the mistress of the place, Mrs. Caldwell. He'd send for Callie from farther south where she lived with his parents and other sister once he had secured the rooms. She, too, wanted to be away from their stepfather, Otto Klein.

Though, admittedly, his stepfather had been good for his mother and a decent provider, Clay did not think of him fondly. Not after the way he'd forced him to marry Alice and jilt the one true love of his life, something he'd kicked himself for hundreds of times over the past seven years. Sure, he'd made the decision to go along with it for a number of reasons, including a promise he'd made to his father...but he wasn't so sure he'd do it again if given a chance to go back in time.

Would he be able to set things right with Gladdie and win her over while he was living here? He'd never find the answer to that question if he didn't try. After writing a letter to his uncle, who now lived in Louisville but kept in touch with folks from Lexington, he'd managed to find out Gladdie had never married—the main reason he'd purchased Blue Acres and returned to Lexington.

This inn out in the countryside adjacent to his new property would be much better than the boardinghouse in the city. The children needed fresh air, and he needed to be close enough to Gladdie. When the construction crew finished building their new home, they could move into it. But that would be a few months from now. He and the children needed somewhere to live until then, and Lottie Belle Country Inn & Board-inghouse was the perfect place.

If he squinted, he could make out the scaffolding set up along the front of his limestone mansion. No windows yet, but he could now see the progress instead of reading about it in reports from the construction manager. After inheriting the entire Parker holdings and all of Alice's estate, at least he'd be able to afford the very best of everything for Olympia—whom he fondly called Ollie and sometimes Olive—and Emery. And Gladdie, if she'd ever give him a chance.

Only one thing made sense to him. Maybe the Lord had been at work to bring about a change in his situation. Was God giving him a chance to finally marry the only woman he'd ever truly loved?

He turned back to the door in time to see it swing open. Expecting Delia, but seeing someone else instead, he held his breath.

"May I help you?" A lady wearing a black dress with a white apron stood on the other side of the door, inspecting him with a raised brow. A household employee?

"Yes, I'm looking to rent three rooms for a few months. Someone in town said your place has plenty of fresh air for children and a big yard to explore. They said I should ask to speak with Mrs. Delia Williams." He wouldn't offer his name lest Delia turn him away before hearing him out.

The uniformed lady nodded. "Wait right here, please."

The door remained ajar while the woman, perhaps in her fifties, disappeared and then returned about a minute later, beckoning him inside. She led him to the kitchen where Delia paused her writing from a seat at the kitchen table. Looking up at him, she gasped.

"Clay! Is that you?"

She hesitated but then rose, her expression unreadable beyond wide eyes and a mustered half smile. Had Gladdie failed to mention her encounter with him a few days ago? Maybe they were busy and hadn't had a chance to talk. That might be a point in his favor.

"Yes, it's me. Nice to see you again. It's been a few years." He returned a warm smile, turning his hat in his hands. Would she ask him to leave once she heard his request? Did he detect a lukewarm welcome?

"That it has. Do have a seat." Delia closed her notebook and set it aside. Then she waved toward the table, indicating an empty chair. "M-may I offer you some coffee or tea?"

"Coffee sounds great. Black, thank you." He sat in the indicated place. If only Gladdie Lyndon would show him a little of the same grace as her sister displayed, but what else did he expect after breaking her heart? He deserved whatever he had coming and couldn't blame Gladdie.

Delia slid a steaming mug toward him and sat in her chair again with a cup for herself. "What brings you to Kentucky after all these years, and specifically to Lottie Belle?"

He drew in a deep breath and sighed, eager to set the record straight. He may as well tell her the whole truth, or as much of it as he could. His pride kept him from telling her everything, as did some complex situations. "I'm looking to rent three rooms while I re-establish a home in Lexington. Folks in town said to check here since it would be nice for the children to be in the countryside. I've returned from New York to make up for something that never should have happened and set things right with Gladdie. Circumstances beyond my control made our plans go awry."

"I thought there must be a reasonable explanation. I tried to help my sister understand, but oh, Clay, she was heartbroken." Delia closed her eyes and shook her head. "She's never been the same since..."

It sounded as though Gladdie had taken the situation even harder than he'd guessed she would, a fact that made him deeply sad. But how could he discuss private matters about his sister Cora with Delia? Maybe best to only mention Alice for now, and even that, he'd have to limit. He drew in another deep breath, nodding. "I was forced to marry Alice Parker to save her from some trouble. Long story short, now that I'm widowed, I have a chance to start again—hopefully, with Gladdie by my side. I know I'll have to work hard to earn her love and trust again, but it is my desire to win over the woman I never stopped loving all these years."

"You were in New York all this time?" Delia's mouth gaped open. "I mean, we'd heard you married Alice Parker, the senator's daughter. We had no idea where you went. Too many conflicting rumors. Someone said you were in Boston. Others said Richmond, Kentucky, or Virginia. And someone suggested New York, but we gave up trying to guess."

The Parkers owned mines in various states. It made

sense that folks had heard different rumors. Delia eyed him with her big chocolate-colored eyes and then leaned forward, but her eyes resembled Gladdie's so much, he had to remind himself that this woman was her sister. Would he ever have a chance to tell the woman he loved what had transpired that night when he'd been forced to miss the train?

"Clay, why don't you start at the beginning? What happened the night you were supposed to marry Gladdie in clandestine?"

Great. He should have known Delia would put him on the spot before he even had a chance to talk with Gladdie...

Twenty minutes later, Clay finally seemed to have satisfied Delia's curiosity. Maybe she would let him sum up now. "Suffice it to say, there were people I had to protect, but it's my hope that once I've had a chance to explain everything to Gladdie, knowing how compassionate she is, she'll come to understand. Since Alice passed away giving birth to our third child, I've now been widowed for a year. It's a chance for new beginnings."

"I'm so sorry to hear this." Delia's lashes fluttered down, and she clasped a hand to her heart. Opening her eyes, her brows arched. "May I ask, did the infant survive?"

He shook his head and looked down at his coffee. "No, sadly. I had to lay them both to rest."

"Oh, Clay...how terrible." Delia sighed. "I pray my sister will find empathy in her heart for your situation. Once you've given her more details, of course."

"I'm doing my best to go on, despite the circumstances. I keep thinking all of the losses can lead to a second chance for Gladdie and me." He clamped his mouth shut. It made him uncomfortable to speak of sorrowful things.

"I sense a spark of hope too. Surely, with time, patience, and hard work, you may be able to win her over." She reached across the table and patted his hand.

Would all that he had shared be enough to convince Delia to rent those rooms to him? Perhaps he should not press her too hard. He'd already stated his request. "Thank you for listening."

Delia bit her lower lip. "You do realize what you're asking of me, right, Clay? You're the person who stole my sister's joy. She may have forgiven you, but it doesn't mean she'll welcome you back into her arms. As her sister, I have to remain loyal to her wishes, whatever they are. Family is family. I may have started a rift between my sister and me, simply for speaking to you."

He nodded and then bent his head, clasping a hand around his coffee cup. "I know. I'm not expecting this to be easy. I appreciate the risk you're taking by even talking with me."

"Well, then, now that I've heard a small glimpse into

what happened, you do understand, I'll have to ask my sister before I can agree to rent three rooms to you. And then my husband, Jake. I realize you'll eventually be our neighbor, since you've purchased Blue Acres."

"I look forward to hearing your decision." Did she realize how much rested on her answer? What if Gladdie said no? He might not see her very often, except for a glimpse of her now and then when he visited the construction site of his new home.

"I can't imagine Gladdie will jump up and down for joy about that. We've all been wondering who was building the mansion there. But just because you have some good reasons for what happened—particularly this bit about you protecting other people—it doesn't mean my sister will be ready for any of this or agree to us regularly associating. I mean, I'm just trying to prepare you for the worst, in case she is adamantly opposed."

Clay shifted in his seat, and the chair creaked a bit under his weight. "I figured you'd say that. Maybe Gladdie will consider the fact that I was only nineteen when all of this happened. I didn't have much of a choice in the matter. Otto, my stepfather, ruled my mother's household with an iron fist. There were other factors too. Things I can't share now...but maybe someday."

"Well, you may need to share all of the details with her sooner if you want Gladdie to understand. A heart can only suffer so much in complete darkness and silence, you know? Many times, she hoped for a letter of explanation from you, and when one never arrived..." Delia rose from her seat. "Her heart was broken in two. She hasn't been the same since returning from Richmond that day. It took weeks to get her to eat again, and much longer for her to engage with society. The bubbly, easygoing, fun-loving Gladdie has never truly returned."

Hearing how all of his actions had affected Gladdie made him more determined than ever to find a way to make things right. But one part of what Delia said drew his brows down low. "I did send a letter. Didn't she receive it?"

She rested her hands on the back of her chair. "No, she didn't receive it."

"Yes, I sent it a few weeks after settling in Lyon's Creek, New York." What had happened to his letter if Gladdie never received it?

"Well, that's troubling. But still..." Delia bristled a bit, standing up taller. "Between not receiving your letter and all those years of wondering what happened, let's just say, it was a very dark time for her. And Clay, I'm not so sure if she'll be happy about the idea of raising Alice Parker's children, either, if you're as serious about marrying her as you say."

"I am very serious about marrying her, if she'll have me, and I do seem to remember how much she loved children, particularly orphans. I have a feeling once she meets them and has a chance to get to know them,

they'll love her as much as she'll come to love them."
Was it wishful thinking on his part?

"Well, to be honest, Jake and I have enjoyed becoming the parents of his nieces. Although, that was a different situation. His nieces are the daughters of his beloved sister, not a woman who absconded with one's intended. But who knows?" She shrugged. "Maybe Gladdie will fall in love with your...did you say Olympia and...?"

"Emery," he supplied. "Olympia, and we call her Ollie. And sometimes Olive, for short."

"Darling nicknames. Yes, my sister does have a weak spot for children. She's never given up her dream of having a school someday for orphans and the under-privileged. But maybe for now, I won't mention the chil-dren unless she asks me why you need three rooms. It may be better to reintegrate into her life a little at a time. You can explain about them when you feel the time is right." Delia crossed the kitchen to the peg on the wall near the back door and reached for her straw hat.

She began pinning the hat in place, talking while she headed toward the hall. "Bring your coffee and come with me to the front sitting room, Clay. You can wait there until I return. You may want to peruse the newspaper while I'm at Velvet Brooks."

Goodness, she spoke a mile a minute. Hadn't Delia been the shy one? She didn't seem so shy anymore.

More confident. All grown up. Very gracious, the same as Mrs. Lyndon.

Clay picked up the coffee and dutifully followed Delia into the hall, passing another uniformed lady who was heading to the kitchen. Probably the cook.

A little girl of about two years met them in the hall and clung to Delia's skirts. Her daughter, perhaps?

"No, Dora. You'll have to wait here with the nanny, but I'll be back in a short while." Delia reached down to console the whimpering child, urging a smile when she tapped the girl softly on the nose.

The elderly lady who'd answered the front door emerged from a room across the hall and picked up Dora.

"There you are, Leonora," Delia said. "Let me introduce you to our guest. Clay, this is Nanny Philips, and this is my daughter, Isadora. We also have Ruby, Ella, and Mary coming home from school shortly."

Jake nodded and smiled. Four children for Olive and Emery to play with would be ideal while they waited to move into their own home, since he'd uprooted them from all they knew in New York. All so he could pursue his own dreams for the first time in his life, although he hadn't sold their home in Lyons Creek. They could still visit friends and inspect the mines whenever needed, though he'd left competent men in charge.

Delia opened the door and stood framed in the threshold. "If you need anything, Nanny usually reads to the children in the library this time of day. And cook is making beef stew for dinner. If Gladdie doesn't ask me to throw you out, you're welcome to join us."

Clay exchanged nods and a greeting with the nanny and a smile with Dora, but before he could utter his thanks to Gladdie's sister or respond about dinner, Delia had wrapped herself in a shawl and hurried out onto the porch. The door closed, and the nanny returned to the library with the child in her arms. He took his coffee to the sitting room and sank into an armchair.

His fate was in Delia's hands now. Or maybe God's, if He cared any. No time to debate that age-old issue that kept creeping up in his heart and mind each time someone died.

Would Gladdie at least permit Delia to allow him to live here until the construction finished on his house? He supposed he could pray for favor. Back when he'd agreed to continue attending church with Alice, he'd heard others testify that asking for favor actually worked. Something like *ye have not because ye ask not* came to mind.

Closing his eyes as another wave of remorse swept him for the pain he'd caused the youngest of the Lyndon sisters, he had no choice but to pray and hope for the best. He bowed his head and mustered up a prayer, something he'd only done a handful of times in recent months. Funny how he'd stopped praying a few months after being forced to marry Alice and only resumed after she died. But the Lord had stirred his heart with all of these recent changes. Was hope springing to life once again?

Unfortunately, in helping Alice and Cora, he'd broken Gladdie's heart...along with his own. He simply had to find a way to make everything right.

CHAPTER FIVE

I knew well enough that one could fracture one's legs
and arms and recover afterward, but I did not know that
you could fracture the brain in your head and recover
from that too.
—Vincent Van Gogh

MARCH 5, 1908
VELVET BROOKS

Gladdie fought off a chill for as long as possible
and finally rose from Pa's desk to add a few more
logs to the fire. She arranged the wood just right with
the poker, causing some sparks to fly up the chimney
until a steady blaze ensued. The last few days of thun-
derstorms had brought on colder weather, but at least
she'd managed one horseback ride when the sunshine
had come out from hiding. Occasionally, her mind

returned to the encounter with Clay in town, a source of perpetual agitation.

She had managed to divest herself of shock and anger after spending some time in prayer and drowning her sorrows in several steaming cups of chamomile tea. What now remained was a mix of curiosity, frustration, and in truth, a pinch of ire that he had dared to return to Lexington.

What could he possibly want? To rekindle friendships, she supposed. And since she couldn't do a single thing to stop it, she would have to do everything in her power to avoid him. How many times had she come to this conclusion in the past few days? Seven…eight times? She shook her head. She really must stop obsessing over his return.

The thud of the screen door closing and footsteps in the hall caused her to stand up straighter and sigh as she shelved her thoughts for later. Voices carried to her ears. Delia speaking with Martin? A few taps on Pa's library door sounded before it creaked open. A glance over her shoulder revealed her sister peeking inside.

"Martin told me you were in here after I let myself in. Goodness! What on earth are you wearing?" After she closed the library door and turned back to take in Gladdie's appearance, Delia's mouth dropped open.

Gladdie returned the poker to its stand, then smiled and swiveled from one side to the other, finally turning all the way around, holding her arms out. "Jodhpurs. Do you approve?"

Delia's eyes widened. She tilted her head, crossed her arms, and then nodded. "Yes, I do. I wonder if Jake would."

"I'm sure. The fellas in the barn think they are great for riding horses." Gladdie crossed to sit behind Pa's desk and finish the last two entries in his ledger so she could be done with the desk portion of her work for the day. She'd had to pay the farrier for new horseshoes, and she'd sent a payment to Pa's doctor. The bank account did not look good, but she couldn't mention it and cause her sister to fret, not in her condition. At least they'd received a timely payment for one of the horses Red had trained for the upcoming racing season.

"Perhaps so, but I don't think the world is ready for you to wear them anywhere else. What did you call them again?" Delia eyed the warm fire and the tea tray. She seated herself in one of the chairs before the hearth, smoothing her skirts.

Martin tapped on the door.

"Come in," Gladdie called out.

"You'll be needing an extra teacup and saucer for Delia. I'll just add it to the tray, Miss Gladdie." Martin waited for her to nod, and when he'd finished the thoughtful task, he hurried out of their way.

"Where were we?" Gladdie inquired.

"You were telling me what you called those, um...?" Delia pointed to Gladdie's lower half.

Gladdie giggled. "Ah, yes. Jodhpurs. I made them myself. I saw them in a fashion plate and purchased a pattern by McCalls at Mama's seamstress shop at Christmastime. I'm very pleased with the result."

"You always were innovative." Delia smirked as she selected a cookie and nibbled the edge.

Gladdie finished her entries and closed the ledger, joining her sister in the two leather chairs. "What brings you to Velvet Brooks in the rain? The girls will be coming home from school soon. Is everything all right?"

"Clay Grinstead has shown up on my doorstep."

Why did she find her mouth dropping open so often these days? Gladdie spluttered for a moment before getting actual words out. "Clay is on your doorstep? What on earth for?" Recovering, she shook her head and pressed hands to her temples. "I confess with a great deal of lament to having seen him racing Thaddeus through town on Monday. Unfortunately, it seems he has returned to Lexington to haunt me forever. I do wish he would mind his own business."

"So you won't be too terribly surprised to discover that he is the mystery owner of Blue Acres, and at this very minute, he is sitting in our front room, waiting for your answer as to whether or not I can rent him three rooms at Lottie Belle until construction is finished on the monstrosity of a mansion he's building." Delia folded her hands on her lap and bit her lower lip.

"What? *He's* the one who purchased Blue Acres?" Gladdie's mouth dropped open...again. Catching herself, she snapped it shut. Why did he need three rooms? She wouldn't inquire about that yet. She had to absorb the fact he was about to become a neighbor, of all things!

Delia nodded, her brown eyes bright with hope. Why did her sister look so eager?

Shaking her head, Gladdie reached for the teapot to pour more chamomile tea into two cups, thankful Martin had delivered a fresh pot before her sister's arrival. The butler had remembered her instructions to only bring flavors that would calm her nerves until further notice. "He actually asked me to attend the Sullivan Ball with him. Can you believe the audacity? And he was racing his horse against Thaddeus and one of his prized mounts to secure an invitation."

"Why doesn't it surprise me to hear of Thaddeus racing? And yes, after speaking to Clay, I can believe he is quite determined to win your affection again." Delia wore a sly, encouraging smile.

Did her sister think she could just let that man walk into her life again? That she should truly consider him after all the years of pain and sorrow? Not to mention the fact that Clay could not be trusted. She tilted her head to one side and, with a good deal of reluctance, passed a cup of tea to Delia. "I don't know why you're smirking. It's my worst nightmare. Why couldn't he have stayed away?"

Delia sipped her tea and said nothing more. How could she remain so calm? Calm as a cucumber. Apparently, her sister considered this good news. Had Clay given her some sort of excuse for his behavior in hopes of obtaining sympathy?

Gladdie released a sigh and lifted the teacup, muttering, "I just can't understand why he has returned from wherever he was—"

"New York."

"—much less purchased the farm right next door."

"All steps to win you back."

"Win me back?" What a preposterous idea.

Delia bit her lower lip before adding, "He said he never stopped loving you."

The plot thickened. So Clay had returned to the area to pursue her...after all these years. Could it be true, and if it was, could she ever return his love? It hardly seemed possible...

Her sister sipped more tea and maintained a stiff posture, as though she was wearing fine silk instead of her...cleaning duster? "I think you should consider attending the ball with him. He seems very repentant and offered a reasonable explanation of what happened when he failed to meet you at the train. He said his stepfather forced him into marriage with Alice to protect some people, along with other reasons which he couldn't divulge—at least, not to me. Perhaps he will tell you. He seems to consider it the biggest mistake of his life."

Oh, he did, did he? How had the man so easily swayed her sister? Gladdie fought down ire—and ridiculous visions of herself marching across the street, waving a shotgun about, and telling Clay Grinstead to saddle up his beautiful horse and go back to wherever he came from.

She huffed. "Well, that doesn't change my mind. I suspected those men had something to do with it. But Clay was a man at nineteen. He knew exactly what he was doing when he abandoned me. I'm not going to any ball with him." Gladdie shoved her teacup back on the table, making it clatter. "Do whatever you feel you must regarding the rental. I'm sure you and Jake need the money. Three rooms is a lot of income."

Delia released a gusty sigh. "Thank you. You're right. We could really use the income, and it would be steady until construction is completed on his mansion. Several months' worth, if I'm estimating correctly. Our girls are all overdue for new shoes and dresses, and with the baby on the way..."

Gladdie waved her hand, not meeting Delia's eyes. "Yes, well, I wouldn't want to see the girls suffer because you turned him away. Though I should tell you to throw him out on his ear, if I had my druthers."

"Gladdie..."

Delia's wheedling tone wouldn't soften her. Gladdie raised her chin. "You can visit me here at Velvet Brooks if you wish to see me. I will avoid setting foot on Lottie Belle for the duration of his stay."

"What about Mary's birthday party?" Delia leaned forward.

"I don't know. I must avoid putting myself in the

same room with that man whenever possible." Life had suddenly become far more complicated. Gladdie chewed her lip. "You might consider hosting the party here."

Delia's hand moved to her growing abdomen. "I hope you'll find a way to come. Mary would be heartbroken without you there."

Hadn't she heard Gladdie offer to host the party at Velvet Brooks? "I'll think about it, but only so long as Clay isn't there. You'll have to choose your guests wisely." Gladdie kept her gaze on the bookshelves in Pa's library. Delia and Jake were already asking a great deal of her to permit the man to rent rooms from them, but to attend a birthday party with him as one of the guests seemed out of the question. "What does Mary want for her birthday? Perhaps I can send my gift in advance. Does she still want those things called crayons?"

"Yes, all she talks about is having a box of crayons from Binney & Smith. I guess they come with five colors and cost five cents a box." Delia fussed with her sleeve. "But I do hope you will consider—"

"Those are the ones I purchased. And a notebook with drawing paper." Gladdie had wrapped the present in some brown paper and tied it with a silk ribbon.

Her sister set her teacup aside. "Listen, Gladdie. Like it or not, Clay is going to be a neighbor. Jake is building Mary a dollhouse as a surprise, and you'll want to see the look on her face when she sees it. I do hope you'll come to the party."

"I'll cross that bridge when I get to it." She'd heard enough about the man who'd jilted her for one day. Gladdie tilted her head and forced a smile, signaling her second attempt to change the topic. "Tell me how you've been. Have you felt better lately?"

"Oh, it seems all I ever do is fight morning sickness and take afternoon naps. I fall asleep sitting up at this stage." Delia straightened and rubbed her neck. "I had hoped to finish a story for the *Lexington Gazette*, but I don't even have the energy to write. And right now, I need to get back..."

Ah, yes. To Clay, whom she'd left waiting in her parlor. Gladdie's expression soured.

"But before I go, tell me about Lady M, the mystery horse."

Gladdie couldn't help but brighten. "After reading her paperwork, we discovered she has some champion bloodlines. Red has been working his wonders. She's almost ready to put to the test on the track. Hopefully soon, she'll let him and Charlie saddle her and allow Charlie to ride without throwing him off. How they got her from New York without ever saddling her..."

Wait a minute. Gladdie's report faded into stunned silence as her mouth fell open yet again.

Hadn't Delia said Clay had been living in New York?

CHAPTER SIX

<blockquote>
We must develop and maintain the capacity to forgive.
He who is devoid of the power to forgive is devoid of the
power to love.
—Martin Luther King, Jr.
</blockquote>

MARCH 6, 1908
VELVET BROOKS

Clay could have hugged Delia when she brought the news that Gladdie would not stand in his way. Along with Olympia and Emery, he moved into the third floor at Lottie Belle Country Inn & Boardinghouse the very next morning after dispatching a telegram to his sister, Callie, telling her to come on ahead. He'd also purchased some items for Gladdie. Didn't every lady enjoy receiving flowers and chocolates? Would she consider them a peace offering of sorts?

Once settled in, with a little help from a housemaid to unpack their trunks, he took the children on a walk to assist them in finding their way around Lottie Belle. Jake had even let Clay park his shiny red Ford Model S Roadster in the carriage house and stable his horse in the barn. He'd introduced him to Hercules, his next great champion horse, sired by a Preakness winner horse he called Horizon.

Until his previous nanny joined them from New York, Callie had volunteered to look after Ollie and Emery. They could be a handful, and he wouldn't deny her offer. After the walk and introductions to everyone in the household, he settled the children in with Dora and Nanny Philips to eagerly await the return of Ruby, Ella, and Mary from school, turning his attention to convincing Gladdie to permit him to escort her to the Sullivan Spring Ball. He had much to make up for where Miss Gladys Lyndon was concerned.

Armed with a box of chocolates from the bakery and white carnations with painted pink edges from the florist, he crossed Cornflower Road on foot and lifted the knocker at Velvet Brooks with every ounce of courage he could marshal.

He'd adjusted his tie three times already, and it still seemed too snug. Would his musky cologne overpower her? Would she notice the shaving cut under his chin from that morning...or be able to tell he'd redone his side part three times to impress her?

The door opened a little more than a quarter of the way. A butler dressed in a black suit—Martin, as he recalled—poked his head out. "Hello. May I help you?"

Why couldn't he get his tongue to move? Was it because the servant hadn't recognized him yet?

"Oh, I know you." Martin tilted his head to one side. "You're...you're Clay Grinstead. The young man who jilted our dear Gladdie." A sneer twisted his face.

Clay stiffened but held his tongue. Given the mature age indicated by the beginning wisps of white and gray streaking the man's hair, he should be respectful.

"A young man no longer, I should say." Martin lifted his chin with some degree of disdain in his wary eyes. "I doubt very much if the lady of the house will agree to speak with you."

This wasn't going well at all, but Clay managed to limit his bristling and find his tongue. "The lady of the house...?" Was Martin referring to Gladdie or Mrs. Lyndon? Hadn't Delia said Mrs. Lyndon was in South Carolina, aiding Mr. Lyndon's recovery following his stroke? Had Gladdie's parents returned? If so, he might find himself in hot water where they were concerned, but wouldn't Delia have mentioned it if they'd come home?

"The mistress is not here presently, and under ordinary circumstances, if she *were* here, she would insist upon knowing the nature of your call. All I can tell you is she is..." The butler clamped his mouth shut as if taking time to choose his words. "...away. Miss Gladys Lyndon is now the lady of the house, and I doubt she'll have time to converse. She is quite busy today." His gaze traveled to the items Clay held. "I assume you are here to call upon her, despite the fact she is otherwise engaged."

Clay swallowed and forced words past the sudden tightening of his throat. "Otherwise...engaged?" Had Delia withheld some very pertinent information from him?

Martin let out a soft, exasperated breath, as if unwilling to answer. "Baking for the orphanage." After he spoke, his mouth formed a flat line.

Relief rushed through Clay. "Ah, yes." That did sound like his Gladdie, always thinking of those less fortunate than herself. Always compassionate, espe-cially to children and orphans. She just didn't have any compassion for him at present, but in time, with a lot of prayer, he could bring her around. Clay stood up taller and cleared his throat. After all, he couldn't let this pipsqueak give him such a dressing down. "Martin, understandably, you are loyal to the household. Just tell Gladdie that Clay would like a word." He should use his manners. "Please."

The butler gave him an ogling evil eye along with a reluctant sigh. "One moment. Wait here." Then he closed the door, quite firmly.

Clay blinked and jerked his head backward at the

rebuff. He shuffled the flowers and the box of chocolates. Loosening his tie again, he summoned patience. This was going to be a long haul. Clearly, where the Lyndon household was concerned, he had a reputation to remedy.

～

Gladdie stopped kneading the mound of bread dough and stood still at the kitchen worktable, blinking. "C-Clay is here?" Her mouth hung open. Why did that keep happening?

Martin nodded, his expression revealing how reluctant he'd been to deliver the message. "I told him you were baking for the orphanage and very busy today. Shall I send him away?"

Grace turned from washing lunch dishes and Willamena paused in mixing up her pie to watch Gladdie, silently awaiting her response.

Nothing would please her more than to send Clay packing. She chided herself for not having the foresight to have expected this. The efficient butler had done his job well, reminding her she had the perfect excuse to avoid accepting the caller. She opened her mouth to do just that when Grace crossed from the sink basin to stand at one end of the worktable, pointing and waving a wooden spoon at her as if it were the finger of Eleanor Lyndon or God Himself.

"Now Miss Gladdie, mind you are as gracious as

your mother would be to that man. Regardless of his past shenanigans, he was just a scrawny teenager back then." Her voice was unwavering. "I remember him as a hardworking, fun-loving boy who adored you. Everybody loved him around here until he tried to run off with you, and that over a decade ago. I'm sure he's a fine gentleman now. Matured by two children, recently widowed, and very wealthy. Don't you go tweaking his nose." Grace returned to the sink to deposit the spoon on the stack of cleaned and drying plates and utensils before plunging her hands into the soapy water for another dish.

Two children? Why hadn't the thought of him having children entered her mind? No wonder he needed to rent three rooms. A twinge of jealousy about Alice giving him children and irritation that Delia hadn't mentioned this detail caused her mouth to clamp shut. At the same time, a wave of curiosity about his children swept over her. Were they sweet, inquisitive, and fun-loving in the way she remembered their father?

Gladdie sighed and resumed kneading the bread. She and Clay surely had another confrontation coming at some point. Maybe today was that day. She kept her head bent over the dough. "I suppose seeing him cannot be prevented forever. Show him into the kitchen until I finish getting these next two loaves into the oven."

Her stomach knotted. Why couldn't this man disappear from her life? Hadn't he done enough harm the first time around?

"I'll put the tea on." Willamena wiped her hands on her apron as she crossed to the stove and began adding more wood to heat the kettle.

Really? Just like that, Clay was invited to tea? Why didn't they advise her to have Martin send him packing? Shrugging, Gladdie nodded toward the butler. She couldn't argue with the women who kept Velvet Brooks running smoothly.

The jubilation in Martin's eyes faded as he glanced around the room. He had probably been eager to exercise his authority. Everyone knew he took his post at the front door seriously, ready to protect their privacy at all costs.

Finally, he blinked, then stiffened his shoulders and gave a curt nod. "I'll return with your guest in a moment."

Gladdie suppressed a groan. This was not the time or setting she would have chosen for her next encounter with Clay, although she'd been wondering if he could possibly have something to do with Lady M. That was the least of what she needed to ask him, but how could she be frank with him in front of the staff? And here she was, wearing an old work apron, with bits of hair straggling down and sticking to her face. Soon enough, he'd see her outside painting fences. Would he presume Velvet Brooks was so understaffed that she must participate in menial tasks?

Thankfully, she hadn't worn her jodhpurs today, though maybe it would be nice to show him her modern and unconventional side.

Well, in truth, there was no reason for any of her worries about appearances. She'd offer him a cup of tea and then politely ask him to forget about her. Would he respect her wishes?

~

After the longest several minutes of Clay's life, Martin returned and finally granted Clay entrance. "She said you may see her in the kitchen. Follow me."

Clay nodded with a sigh and stepped inside the charming farmhouse. He'd always loved it here. Familiar with the outdoor kitchen Willamena frequently used in the summertime, he'd only entered the kitchen inside the main house for Velvet Brooks a handful of times, and he assumed that was where the longtime employee would now lead him. Would it look the same as he remembered? And at least he'd remembered the cook's name.

He followed the butler through the hall, past the same beautifully polished staircase with its wooden banisters, into the music room with the shiny baby grand piano. They turned to the left, but he glanced to his right, remembering the sitting room where he'd once kissed Gladdie's cheek. Flashes of memories flooded in, reminding him of many a summer day spent here with the one true love of his life...when he hadn't been busy helping his uncle a few miles away at his former farm, or in the city with his mother and sisters. They hadn't had employees and servants as the Lyndons had, and he and his sisters had worked hard to help keep things running after his father had died, until his mother had married Otto. The financial situation had improved a little then. He'd give Otto that much.

The butler held the kitchen door open as delicious scents wafted in the air, permitting him to enter. He spotted Gladdie at once, kneading dough at the worktable in the center. She wore her shiny brown locks gathered up in one of those fashionable topknots ladies favored, a pinafore-style apron over her white shirtwaist and black skirt, sleeves rolled up, her head bent over her work. Some loose curls fell around her face as she concentrated on her task. Pretty as a picture, even with a bit of flour dotting her nose.

"Mr. Clay Grinstead to see Miss Gladys Lyndon," the servant announced.

Gladdie punched the dough, refusing to look up at Clay. "Thank you, Martin."

Was he dreaming? Why did it feel as though they were the only ones in the room, though others were present, seemingly focused on their duties. He'd waited for this moment for so long, for the chance to speak to her. Somehow, he'd never imagined addressing her in the kitchen.

What he wouldn't give to see her smile at him! But she continued kneading and punching the mound of dough on the table, ignoring his presence as the testy butler slipped away, leaving him standing there awkwardly.

Gladdie wiped a corner of her forehead with her upper arm, finally glancing up at him. "I'm very busy, as you can see, Clay. In fact, I was tempted to decline seeing you, so if you would come right to the point... What brings you to Velvet Brooks?" She arched a brow but instantly returned her focus to her work.

He didn't answer. Partly because she punched the dough with enough force to knock all of the yeast completely out of it, causing his lips to press into a firm line and his brows to lower. He recovered quickly and took one step closer to the table. "Careful there, you might hurt the bread." His voice came out soft, laced with mild amusement.

Willamena and the other servant turned and looked at him, a smirk on the cook's face.

Gladdie barely glanced at the flowers and candy he placed on the edge of the worktable. "These are for you."

Her gaze traveled to his peace offering and then up at him. Did he detect fire in those big brown eyes?

She spun around, opened the oven door a few steps away, and swiped a folded linen from her shoulder, using it to pull two loaves of freshly baked bread from the oven. The golden-brown tops on the loaves made his mouth water. Gladdie employed a table knife to loosen the bread from each pan. Turning each pan upside down, one at a time, she slid the baked goods onto the table for cooling beside some other loaves. Would she be taking several of those to the orphanage? How often did she do such good works? Questions he hoped to ask her one day, if she'd ever let him into her world.

What else could he say? Another quick glance around the kitchen revealed Willamena rolling pie dough at some other counter under the cupboards. Grace—yes, that was her name—washed dishes at the sink basin, her sleeves rolled up. Gladdie turned and stirred a pan of what appeared to be cherry preserves at the stove, then swirled a different spoon through a savory stew on the back burner.

Best to say what he required and hope for the best. "I only wanted a private word with you when you have a moment."

Swiping a few stray curls from her face, she returned to the worktable and began forming the remaining dough into two more loaves, making quick work of it. In what seemed mere seconds, she placed each loaf into a pan, slid them into the oven, and turned back to face him while wiping her hands on a linen.

"Grace, I'll have tea in the sitting room with Mr. Grinstead, if you'd be so kind as to prepare a tray." She untied her apron as she spoke.

No words to him, but at least she'd finally said

something. A wave of relief swept over him. Tea? He hadn't expected her to cooperate that far.

Grace dried her hands, crossing from the sink to the stove and reaching for the kettle. "Yes ma'am, I'll see to it, and I'll put the flowers in some water."

"Thank you, Grace." Gladdie tossed her apron aside and slipped between the worktable and stove, then moved toward the door leading to the music room. "Clay, follow me."

Anywhere.

Grace's words echoed through Gladdie's mind as she led Clay into the sitting room. Best to offer tea and send him on his way as soon as possible. At least with her going by the customs of the day, he would assume they were doing fine at Velvet Brooks. She refused to let him know how difficult things were.

As she and Clay settled into the chairs near the fireplace where her parents usually sat, she couldn't think of a single thing to say. What she wanted to say wasn't fit for polite society, but he remarked on how everything looked just as it used to. So mannerly, when she had to sit on one hand and swallow the idea of slapping him.

"I remember spending many a summer afternoon trying to escape the heat playing checkers and chess in this very room." His gaze traveled to take in the ribbons, cups, and even silk jerseys worn by some of their former jockeys, all displayed nicely behind glass doors in one of Mama's china cabinets. "Do you still play the piano?"

My, how his eyes took in every detail. It pained her to answer him with civility when she would so much rather shout, but as Grace had said, she must behave with kindness and graciousness. "Yes, sometimes I still play."

After releasing a sigh, she bit her lower lip. Why must she carry on as if this man was an old friend? Smoothing her skirts, she toyed with how she might frame the request uppermost in her mind. *Clay, please forget I ever existed.* Or perhaps, *Clay, you must go away and never return. Forget about me.*

How silly that seemed when they would become neighbors after he moved into his mansion.

Grace appeared with a tea tray in the open door. That at least gave Gladdie something to keep her hands busy. She began pouring as soon the efficient lady's maid deposited the tray on the small round table between them and hurried away, though it went against every bone in Gladdie's body to do so. He really did not deserve tea poured from her hand.

When she handed him a cup, he smiled, but she caught him studying her stoic expression, and his smile faded. He set his cup aside. "Gladdie...my dear, sweet Gladiola, I came to ask you to please consider allowing me to be your escort to the Annual Sullivan Spring Ball.

It pains me so that I have hurt the one girl who taught me to smile again after the passing of my brother and father. And I am determined to see a smile return once again to your face as well, and to spend the rest of my days making you happy, if you will please give me that chance."

Was he proposing *and* asking her to the ball? He hadn't called her his Gladiola in ages. She had to admit how nice it sounded to hear his term of endearment once again. But he wouldn't win her over that easily.

When she didn't say anything, he added, "Please say yes."

She could not look into his eyes beyond a brief glance to gauge his sincerity. Not because she would consider his request, but because a wave of curiosity swept over her. Did he truly speak from the heart? He gave every indication it was so. And while she wanted to ask how he was doing and find out more about him, about his feelings on the matter, she wasn't done being angry with him. Would she ever be done with such intensely negative feelings about this man she used to love with her whole heart?

"Clay..." Exasperation surfaced in the mix of emotions welling within her, and she set her teacup aside and reached for the hooped sampler she'd been working on of late. When she finished it, she would stow it in her hope chest with others she had made over the years. This one would not be a gift or be displayed here at Velvet Brooks, but rather would hang in her future home in a particularly pleasing spot. But would she ever have her own home if she continued to refuse to consider marriage?

He leaned forward despite the fact she wouldn't look into his eyes. "Please, don't say no. I cannot accept no for an answer."

"Why should I give you another chance to hurt me? I'm sure I can't think of a single reason to give you that kind of freedom or power, Mr. Grinstead." As she simmered like the stew for tonight's supper, the muscles in her face tightened.

She found the needle, and thankfully, it was still threaded. She didn't think she could manage threading a needle with her eyes misting. She bent her head over the embroidery project and stabbed the needle through the cloth, pulling the blue thread through the fabric. How much she loved the Lord's Prayer, the words she had set out to stitch. But could she truly expect to be forgiven if she didn't fully forgive the man seated beside her?

She'd thought she had forgiven him. And perhaps forgiving did not necessarily include inviting someone to become so close that the individual might cause hurt, pain, and turmoil again. A next time might leave her far beyond repair. But the mere sight of him dredged up the past. Perhaps because they'd never spoken about the way he'd jilted her. She wasn't sure she could ever speak with him about it. Yet why did it seem as if that was exactly where they were headed?

When she stabbed the fabric a third time, he reached across the small tea table between them for her hand, giving her a wary look as he pulled the project gently away and set it aside. "We can't have you stabbing yourself with such a sharp needle…"

Ordinarily, she would have laughed at her actions, but she was steaming. Everything was happening so fast. Instead, she said, "You didn't answer my question."

"Why you should give me another chance?" His gaze softened, his words coming out in a slow, tender, sincere voice. "Because I've never stopped loving you, Gladdie. And because I won't give up just because you say no. And because we belong together. You know it, and I know it. We've always been meant for each other."

She snatched her hand from him, tears welling in her eyes. "No, Clay. I do not know it. I don't believe I belong with someone who breaks his word. I can only ever marry someone like my father, a man who keeps his promises, *if* I marry at all. And since this is a matter which cannot be reconciled, I implore you to forget that I ever existed. Forget about me." There, she'd said it.

One peek at his aghast expression from under her lashes revealed the pain in his eyes.

He shifted in his seat, raking a hand through his blond hair. "You cannot possibly mean those words. I could never forget you, Gladiola. Have I done so much harm that you will never marry anyone? It does not seem possible, but I see that I have done terrible damage. Tell me it isn't irreparable. Surely, we can redeem this situation if we work at it together."

She couldn't let his poetic words deceive her again. He'd always been an avid reader despite a middle-class upbringing with an average public education. But even educated men sometimes failed to abide by the rules of courtship. Apparently, he'd missed the part about loyalty.

She rang Mama's little bell to summon Martin and rose. "I shall thank you in advance for *not* returning and for respecting my wishes." Her vision blurred, and she blinked tears back. *Don't cry. Not yet. Not until he's gone.*

The trusted servant appeared in seconds, eyeing her guest suspiciously.

Clay's chest heaved, and he reluctantly stood, a heavy sigh escaping his lips. "I won't give up, Gladdie. I won't. If it's the last thing I do..."

"Martin, if you will please escort our guest to the front door, he was just leaving." Disregarding Clay's words outwardly, she maintained an indifferent expression. Inwardly, though, she had to admit, the declaration offered a balm after so many years of questioning. But she was nowhere near ready to admit anything of such a personal nature to him.

Despite the sorrow evident in his eyes, she couldn't trust what she beheld there. How could he know the depth of *her* suffering? Those children he now had could have been children he gave her. While he'd had the arms of another woman to hold and caress him, she hadn't had anyone but the Lord, although the Lord was all she had truly needed. He had proven Himself to her. Afflicted and cast aside, she'd had to go on living even without the will to live. But somehow, the Lord had shown her things to do. He'd given her purpose.

And now that she had recovered the will to live, found some bit of purpose for her existence in caring for the orphans and nourishing her dream for a school, she had to protect her heart and future. A future which did not include Clay Grinstead...

Or did it? Because after he'd left with Martin on his heels, when his footsteps faded and the front door closed, why did her heart ache so much? Why did she long for him to take her in his arms and kiss all her wounds away?

Did some part of her still long for this man to love her, even after all of these years? Was God trying to give her a second chance, like Lady M, the horse in their barn? A horse no one had been able to saddle? And goodness...Clay had so completely flustered her that she'd forgotten all about the mystery of the filly. Now that she'd sent him away, would she ever know? More importantly, with the ball only ten days away, had she just closed the door on her second chance with the only man she had ever really loved?

CHAPTER SEVEN

One can get in a car and see what man has made. One must get on a horse to see what God has made.
—Author Unknown

MARCH 7, 1908
LOTTIE BELLE

Clay stepped onto the front porch at Lottie Belle the next morning with a hot cup of coffee, freshly brewed by Delia's cook. Such a nice front porch with a glorious view from where the farmhouse sat atop the crest of a hill that rolled gently to its peak. Not only could he take in the clumps of blue bachelor buttons and pink-and-white star lilies along Cornflower Road, but he could admire thick mounds of purple and pink phlox blooming in the flower beds along the veranda of the farmhouse across the dirt road. One of these days, the city would pave the old dirt road, making it safer for the modern automobile. For now, its natural state held a rustic appeal. But most of all, he took joy in being able to steal glimpses of Miss Lyndon—his Gladiola—taking one of her morning horseback rides.

Clearly, he needed a new strategy to win her over. His first two attempts hadn't been entirely futile, though. They had proven he faced the next great challenge of his life. But what could he try now?

The Kentucky belle presently traversed the lawn of Velvet Brooks on the back of a dapple grey in a full sprint toward the creek that formed part of the dividing line between his property and hers. And she wore some sort of new-fangled ladies' riding pants. He let out a whistle under his breath, careful lest she hear him. Though he very much approved, it wouldn't do to offend her any more than he already had.

He lingered over the coffee, savoring every sip, pondering how to win her hand. He checked his pocket watch. Ollie and Emery would wake in about half an hour, in time for a hearty breakfast served by Delia's cook. In fact, the smell of bacon wafted through the front door screen.

After breakfast, he'd see to it that the children were settled in with Nanny Philips before he drove into the city to pick up Callie at the Lexington train depot. The children planned on a tea party with Dora, one of

Delia's ideas. They would use Ollie's play tea set she'd brought from New York, and Delia's cook had pledged to provide real tea and tiny cakes.

He'd also promised to take them for a ride in the rowing boat on the pond behind the farmhouse, and after, some fishing in the same pond, using some of Jake's fishing poles he'd generously offered. It would give his sister time to unpack and settle into her room at Lottie Belle.

Next, he just had to plan the type of education he would provide for the children. After all, they had both reached school age. He could enroll them in the local public school where Ruby, Ella, and Mary attended. Jake and Delia's three older girls certainly seemed to enjoy their school, and his children needed to make friends with others their age, something a public school education easily provided.

Then again, there was something to be said for limiting one's social interactions and choosing them carefully. Alice had been very clear about her wishes for private tutors, governesses, or private schools. But after seeing how happy Jake's nieces were, he'd begun to lean again toward providing an education more like his own, where ordinary folks were schooled. He'd made a number of friends over the years at the public school he'd attended in Lexington, but Alice's wishes still tugged on him.

Gladdie rode up to the big barn at Velvet Brooks and swung out of the saddle, then led her mount inside.

What would she suggest about the education of his children? If he could ask her, he would.

One more prayer couldn't hurt. After all, Jake led his family in prayer and Bible reading each morning before the girls left for school. The practice seemed to be working for his family. *Lord, if You help me win Gladdie back as my wife, I'll serve You all the days of my life. I'll start taking the children to church again and raise them up to serve You.*

There, he'd said it. Maybe not out loud, but from the heart. And he meant it, too, though he'd just begun to acknowledge that even if God didn't answer his prayer the way he wanted, a recommitment to his Heavenly Father was something he should have done long before now. Had the pain in his heart blinded him before? He mustn't let that ever happen again. God needed to be first in his life.

A few construction workers rumbled in a wagon up the drive toward his future home. Nice to see progress from Lottie Belle's front porch. The sight of construction buoyed his hopes for the future.

His gaze traveled back to Velvet Brooks. Where had Gladdie gone? Ah! There she was. Working hard at something. Painting a long fence that encircled the enormous meadow, a brush in her hand and a container of paint perched on a post. She'd be at that for a while. There were so many fences on that farm, and four-board ones. She'd be painting for days, maybe even weeks.

His eyes widened, and a smile spread across his face as an idea sparked like a sagebrush fire. He could offer assistance around the farm to Gladdie, doing some of the things her father would normally do if he wasn't on the coast, recovering his health. Sad, what Delia had said about Mr. Lyndon's health. Would Gladdie let him help?

Nothing spoke the word *love* like good old-fashioned hard work. And wasn't he a bit weary of sitting behind a desk for years as the vice president of Parker Mines—and now the owner—pushing paper day in and out? It had been exhilarating at first, being offered a senior position at the young age of nineteen by his father-in-law and Alice's grandfather, Judge Parker.

But he wouldn't mind offering a hand to Gladdie. All those years he'd spent helping around his uncle's farm, he'd learned fencing left unpainted would succumb to the elements and end up with mildew. Over time, they would need replaced. Wise of her to paint them before any rot set in. He would certainly enjoy spending time with her, too, even if all she did was glare at him. And he still needed to tell her about Ollie and Emery. Would she be happy to meet them? Would she enjoy seeing Callie again?

If Gladdie wouldn't let him help paint, maybe the men who worked for her father wouldn't mind having an extra hand around the place. Satisfied with his plan, he headed inside, an extra bounce in his step.

"You must let me drive part of the way, Clay. I've always wanted to try driving one of these contraptions, and I never have the opportunity," Callie complained later that morning as the automobile chugged along through the traffic in town once he'd secured her trunk and other items. Unfortunately, the motor was so loud, they had to raise their voices to be heard. At least they had beautiful warm weather for the ride to Lottie Belle.

"Wait until we're out in the countryside. Maybe then." He could understand how being cooped up with Otto and his mother would make a lady anxious for some sort of recreation.

"Thank you. This is going to be so much fun!" His sister turned in her seat to face him, holding onto the dashboard with a gloved hand. "How are you holding up? I mean, since Alice...?"

"I'm all right." He couldn't exactly say he had only ever developed a healthy degree of fondness for Alice. She'd attended his Presbyterian church and they'd grown up in different neighborhoods located close together inside the city limits of Lexington. He'd been born into a lower-middleclass family, while she came from old money. They hadn't been in love as most married couples were. Instead, they'd made the best of what was purely a marriage of convenience. "Thank you for asking. You will remember not to discuss Cora no matter how much you are pressed, if the subject comes up."

"I promise. You know how we both dislike that subject. The gossip that follows seems inevitable. But what exactly do you want me to say if anyone asks?" Callie held a hand to her hat as they rounded a bend in the road and the view began to transform into more of the countryside.

He gripped the wheel tighter, more from the tension the subject of Cora always caused him than anything else. "I don't know. Just say she is doing well and change the subject. Nothing more." That was his plan too. What else could they say? Folks needed to mind their own business.

"What if they ask where she is living?" Callie's brow arched.

"Tell them she's with Otto and mother. The less said, the better." Another bend in the road made them both lean to the right.

"Yes, we must protect Cora. What if they ask where Otto and mother live? What do you want me to say?"

"I've been saying they live in the countryside in southern Kentucky. If you are pressed, then say not too far from Richmond, but do try to keep folks from details they don't need to know." It was the truth and vague enough to keep folks from interfering. If Callie could live up to her word, it would do everyone some good.

"I can do that. She's doing fine, living with Otto and mother in the countryside in southern Kentucky...if they ask." Callie smiled and sat back in her seat. "On another note, is Gladdie speaking to you yet?"

"Not yet, but all in good time. If you encounter her, try to be nice to her no matter how she reacts. It's going to take time." Why did he have a bad feeling gnawing at his gut? If Callie caused any problems, he'd regret permitting her to live with them. Callie possessed a talkative, bubbly nature. Would she spill secrets he preferred to keep quiet? But how would she ever find a husband if he didn't help his sister widen her prospects? She'd been tucked away in the countryside long enough, and though they'd be in the same kind of environment here, at least they knew plenty of folks around Lexington.

"Do you remember my old friend, Aurelia? I can't wait to meet her next week for tea. I called her on the telephone so she didn't know where I was calling from...so you needn't worry. But I'll need a ride into town." She reached for her purse, fishing around for something inside it.

"Sure, fine. Just let me know what day so I can write it on my personal calendar." He hardly remembered Aurelia, but it would probably be good if Callie had a friend around to help keep her occupied.

"You keep a calendar now? How smart and organized you are, Clay." She stopped fussing with the contents of her purse for a moment to arrange her skirts, shifting in her seat to face the road, looking around at the countryside.

"I always write down important dates. I have employees, children, a social calendar, and decisions to be made." He sighed as they rounded another curve. "Then again, maybe I write dates down because I can't remember anything if I don't. I make lists too."

"Well, in all honesty, you being forgetful is not surprising. We did have a difficult childhood. For some reason, I can't remember several years of when we grew up. Can't remember some of my teachers' names, what I received for Christmas or birthdays, or anything at all." Callie resumed rummaging in her purse, producing something ladies called lip balm. She began applying the cosmetic. "Maybe being with you and the children will cheer me up. Bring back some of the missing memory gaps."

He did no more than nod because shifting gears and bends in the road demanded his attention, replying a moment later. "Some of those times were sad. I don't want to remember them. Living through it once was enough for me."

Callie laughed. "You have a point there. We lost our precious little brother and our father. How on earth did we survive?"

"We learned to be strong. And Gladdie taught me to laugh again." Could he count on Callie not to mess things up for him with her?

"Except for Cora. She didn't learn to be strong." She sighed.

Her lament reached the depths of his soul and the pit of his stomach. "Except for Cora," he repeated. Since Callie had grown sentimental, he couldn't exactly remind her one more time to be exceptionally nice to the Lyndons and to be sure to look after his children properly. He'd have to save those things for later. And why did he have the feeling she would need multiple reminders? She'd always been a little featherbrained, and she hadn't had any children of her own yet to look after, but maybe she had learned a few skills from assisting Cora now and then.

She brightened, turning toward him again, this time displaying mischievous eyes and a wide smile. "I am simply overjoyed that you're building a mansion bigger than the one at Sullivan Hill. I can't wait to see it. I always thought the Sullivans were a bit on the uppity side. I thought the Lyndons were, too, until I met Gladdie."

He grinned, glancing at her. "She's wonderful, isn't she?"

Callie laughed. "You are in love, Clay Grinstead!"

He chuckled, nodding. "I've always been in love with Gladdie. And nothing is going to stop me from marrying her this time."

Had she heard him loud and clear? Hopefully, since he'd had to shout it over the rumble of the engine. But something about saying it felt kind of wonderful. Judging by the way Callie laughed, she seemed to understand his intentions.

"If you look to my left, you can see the mansion I'm building."

She leaned over to take it all in, breathing out her admiration. "Oh, my goodness...it is beautiful, Clay!"

The road straightened as they sped past, nearing Lottie Belle, but it was Velvet Brooks that caught his attention as he scanned the lawn for a glimpse of his Gladiola. Maybe he could let Callie take over for the last bit. "Ready to try driving this beast?"

She clasped her hands together. "And how!" Leave it to Callie to use the most nonsensical modern expression possible to express what should be simple agreement.

He shifted into the lowest gear, steering the machine to one side of the road, easing to a stop. After he applied the hand brake lever, they traded places. Callie couldn't stop giggling with glee as she slid into his seat, and he went around to the passenger side.

A short jaunt to Lottie Belle's drive. Harmless enough. Barely an eighth of a mile...

"What does this pedal do?" She pushed on the gas pedal, and the engine roared but didn't move the car forward.

"Careful, now! That's the gas. You'll need to release that lever first." He pointed to the hand brake. "Step on the clutch. All the way to the floor. And with your other foot, step on the gas, lightly. Then let off the clutch a little at a time and give it a bit more gas."

The motor carriage jerked them forward as she

laughed. But when the automobile took off at a remarkable speed, Callie let out a scream.

"Not that much gas!" He probably shouldn't have let her drive.

She laughed again as they shot forward. Would they make it to Lottie Belle in one piece? Maybe they should switch back. Between her laughter, shouting at each other to hear over the motor, the way she brought them to sudden stops and then thrust them forward, and all of the times she drove them into the grass along the edge of the road, Clay spiraled into a state of panic.

"There's Lottie Belle. Turn right!" he hollered over the engine. "Right…" Too late. She'd managed to turn left instead of right. "Brake! Brake!"

No, not a ditch! Clay braced for impact, and Callie screamed as she clung to the wheel, steering them directly into a four-board fence.

Glass shattered, the fence boards tumbled down with a cracking noise, and metal crunched.

CHAPTER EIGHT

A horse never runs so fast as when he has other horses
to catch up and outpace.
—Ovid, Roman poet who lived during the reign of
Augustus

MARCH 7, 1908
VELVET BROOKS

Stunned, Clay blinked a few times, his mouth hanging open as a great deal of steam released from the engine. He climbed out of the conveyance to survey the damage. The shattering glass was due to the left headlight she'd taken out, and the right one did not look as though it was going to last for long, judging by the way it tilted to one side. And the crinkle in the hood made his brows furrow.

At least Callie had managed to find the brake during the crash, bringing them to a stop, though perhaps the ditch and the fence were responsible. For some miraculous reason, the motor to the conveyance still chugged and sputtered. Shouldn't it have died? He'd take it as a sign from God that He'd heard one or more of his recent prayers.

"I'm so sorry, Clay. I don't understand how this happened..." Callie's blue eyes were wide with alarm. "I've broken your machine and the fence."

First things first. "Are you all right? Any broken bones?"

"I'm fine." She sniffed. "But your beautiful machine...it's ruined."

"No, don't cry. I'll have it repaired. I'm just glad you're not hurt." He sat up straighter. "As a matter of fact, you've done me a great favor."

"I have?" She straightened her hat, turning to look at him with bewilderment in her expression.

He rested a hand on the side of the conveyance closest to the hand brake just in case she accidentally stepped on the accelerator pedal. "I've been looking for a good reason to help Gladdie at Velvet Brooks, and now I've got one. I can start by repairing her fence."

His sister offered a weak smile. "I suppose there is a silver lining in that. And I don't seem to have mussed my new hat. We aren't hurt. So there are three positives, but I have my doubts about learning how to drive anytime soon. It's so complicated with all of these pedals and levers."

Somehow, the look on her face made him chuckle. "I can't argue with that. Let's switch places. Maybe we can make it up the drive to Lottie Belle if I can get it to shift into the reverse gear." After Callie slid over, he settled into the driver's seat. "Before your next driving lesson, you need to learn the difference between right and left."

"Oh dear brother, you have a point there. I've never been good at that. Otto is always lecturing me about it." Callie's face wrinkled into a pout.

He'd seen that expression on her face a hundred times. After Clay found reverse, they sputtered up Lottie Belle's lane, parking alongside the front porch. He probably needed to add some water to the engine, judging by the amount of steam gushing out and the whooshing noise as it sizzled and simmered. The motor backfired before he found the button to turn off the contraption, but they'd finally made it to the inn. "Welcome to our new temporary home."

Callie jumped out and dashed around the automobile, lifting her skirts, about to run up the steps leading to the front door. "Hurry, Clay! I can hardly wait to meet Olympia and Emery. I'm an auntie and am simply determined to be the very best auntie in the whole world. I've brought presents too. A toy sailboat for Emery and a trinket box for Olympia."

"Hold on a minute, Callie." He hurried to climb out and stop her, torn between heading back to Velvet Brooks to alert them about what had happened and introductions at Lottie Belle. He desperately needed to inform Gladdie that he would repair her broken fence. But Ollie burst through the door with Emery on her heels, excitement dancing in her blue eyes. Clay raked a hand through his hair. He'd have to rush through settling his sister and then hasten across Cornflower Road. Best to unload the trunk first.

"You're back from the train station!" Ollie's voice rang out. She stopped in her tracks and smiled shyly at his sister. "Is this our Aunt Callie?"

"Yes, I'm your auntie, children. You must be Olympia, and you must be Emery." Callie bent to embrace her niece and nephew. Then she ruffled Emery's brown locks before turning back to Ollie. "What a darling sailor suit, Emery, and such a pretty dress you're wearing, Miss Olympia."

Ollie basked in Callie's praise as she smoothed her dress with its three tiers of ruffles. "Thank you. You may call me Olive or Ollie. Everyone does. Are you going in the rowing boat with us?"

"Whoopie! Is it time to get in the boat?" Emery held up a stick with some string, presumably for fishing, and began dancing around Callie and his sister, jumping up and down every few steps. Had Delia given Emery some string to use with the stick he'd found on the grounds?

Clay couldn't help but smile at these introductions,

but he dreaded telling the children they'd have to delay their fishing plans.

"What's happened to the motor carriage, Father?" Ollie's eyes widened as she gazed past him.

Clay finished hefting the trunk to the door. "About that...we may have to postpone our plans. We've had a little run-in with a fence."

A chorus of groans reached his ears.

"It's my fault, children. I drove your father's beautiful motor carriage into the fence at Velvet Brooks." Callie shook her head as Emery stopped dancing and Ollie continued to stare.

"Callie, let me take your things upstairs. You can unpack and get settled into your room. We're on the third floor, but you'll have a room beside the children. I'll need to ask Jake about borrowing his wagon, and maybe he can tell me where I can purchase some lumber. Children, what do you say about a wagon ride for today? Then we can go boating and fishing after I finish the repairs. With any luck, maybe by tomorrow."

More groans from Emery.

Ollie's eyes brightened. "Yes, let's ride in the wagon. Can I bring my doll?"

"Can I bring my toy soldiers?"

Leave it to Olive to find the bright spot in the new plan. If only Gladdie would look so positively on the turn her day was about to take. Could he hurry across Cornflower Road to speak with Gladdie before she noticed the damage to her fence?

$\sim$

Velvet Brooks

"What was that noise?" Gladdie rose from the writing desk in the dining room and peered through the nearest window, speaking aloud to no one in particular since she had the room to herself. Had some part of the barn roof collapsed? No, that was the unmistakable churning and chugging of a driving machine.

She parted Mama's lace curtain panels. The barn was indeed fine. No sign of an automobile coming up the lane. But there, next to an entire section of her fence splintered and flattened on the ground, sat Clay Grinstead in his shiny red conveyance.

Who was that woman seated behind the wheel? Quite a hat atop her head, smart and fashionable. She might seem a bit familiar, but from this distance, it was hard to say.

No doubt, he'd come around to apologize before the hour was out. And likely, he'd insist upon repairing the severely damaged fence. The modern machine looked in even worse shape. Was it his? Steam billowing out of it and a lopsided headlight nearly made her chuckle as her hand flew to cover her mouth.

Clay walked around the machine to trade places with the lady driver. At least no one had been hurt, but this meant another encounter with him. Would she ever escape him? And did she *want* to keep pushing him away? Perhaps a little less so each time she saw him.

And who was that woman who'd driven the machine into her fence? Had Clay decided to forget her already? Well, she only had herself to blame if so. He had tried. The vase of white carnations where Grace had placed them on the dining room table told Gladdie that much. She'd donated the chocolates to the orphanage along with several loaves of bread and three jars of jam.

Shaking her head, she returned to the desk to finish writing her letter to Pa. But as she updated him about her progress in painting the fencing at Velvet Brooks and the new mare, why did she keep thinking of the woman driving Clay's auto? Her heart ached as she considered the idea of other women flirting with her former beau.

The front screen door slammed, and Martin burst into the room a few seconds later from the front hall. "You'll never guess who just drove into our fence as I was planting those lilac starters Harvey Higginbottom dropped off this morning."

Gladdie glanced up to see the watering can for Mama's flowers in his hands, a spade tucked in a pocket of his handy gardening belt. She bent her head over the letter and finished a swirl on her signature. "Clay Grinstead and a woman wearing a fashionable hat with enough tulle to make Delia turn positively pea green with envy."

"How did you know?" Martin crossed his arms and leaned against the doorframe.

She put her pen down and peeked up at Martin, a smile playing on her lips. "I heard it, too, and went to the window. I thought the sky had fallen, but it was only Clay and that lady, trying to make my life one giant headache." And heartache, she might add.

She folded the letter and reached for an envelope from one of the slots above the drop-down writing leaf. She wouldn't tell Pa they barely had enough to make next month's payroll, or that they had lost another horse-training client, or that she may not have enough paint to finish painting because she'd nearly used the entire supply. She mustn't cause him any alarm or strain to his health, though he surely knew how stressful the month of March could be when it came to having enough funds after a long, hard winter.

If they could harvest the winter wheat and sell some of it, they might squeak by until the Phoenix Stakes, the beginning of the year's racing season. And hopefully, it would be a better racing season than the previous one.

Martin tapped a finger on his chin. "The lady looked a tad familiar to me."

"I'm trying not to care who she is, and from this distance, she could have been almost anyone and we wouldn't know." Gladdie began writing the address for Chesapeake Manor on the envelope.

A knock sounded from the front door, and before

Martin could turn toward the hall and answer, someone stepped inside. Clay wouldn't have arrived that quickly, would he? Nor would he simply walk inside the farmhouse, would he?

"Oh, hello, Carter." Martin took a step into the foyer and angled toward the entrance. "Did you see what happened to our fence on Cornflower Road?"

Phew! Not Clay yet. She should tidy her hair... maybe change into something more elegant. But when had she started caring what Clay thought of her? Was she trying to dress nicely for him...or prove the farm was still as successful as ever? Some of both maybe, in all honesty.

Martin stepped inside the dining room to make space as Carter appeared in the doorway. "I saw it too. I'm sure Clay will make it right. I came to fetch Miss Gladdie for Lady M's maiden run around the track."

Gladdie smiled, thankful for something other than Clay to occupy her mind. "I wouldn't miss it for the world. Does Red think she's ready?"

The trainer believed a horse only needed a little time with a saddle and rider before turning the pair loose for a run on the track. He—and Pa, for that matter —considered it one of the most surefire ways to discover a horse's racing potential.

The groom nodded with a wide smile. "I think she'll break a record. As feisty as she is, under Charlie's hand, we'll see exactly what she's capable of." Only someone as experienced as their jockey had the expertise to handle the temperament of their new mare.

"Let me get my hat." Gladdie placed the letter aside and rose.

She stepped into the hall and pinned her hat in place. She could hardly wait.

A few minutes later, after a brisk walk alongside Carter to the track beyond the horse barn, Gladdie leaned over the rails. She and Carter stood near the finish line at the quarter-mile marker, the groom aiming the pistol he held toward the clouds. Red, stopwatch in hand, took up his place nearby.

Brady Danford straddled a fine stallion named Buttercup Champion, currently their fastest and best. Charlie struggled to hold Lady M behind the starting line. The horse sashayed right and left, making it a challenge for the jockey to maintain his seat.

Bang! Carter fired off a blank while Hank waved a white flag in a downward motion to signify the start of the race. With Charlie digging his heels into Lady M's girth, the startling sound was enough to cause the mare to begin well.

"And they're off!" Hank grinned, stepping up beside them to grip the rails with his large hands. Nathaniel and Red had clicked their stopwatches.

Gladdie held her breath as Charlie and Brady leaned low over their mounts' manes. The horses flew past them toward the first turn, but Lady M was already easing her way to the inside rail and ahead of Buttercup. Around she went, making short work of the remaining distance, falling into an easy pace while gaining an even greater lead.

Red released a whistle as he checked the time on the stopwatch. Was Lady M already breaking records with her initial performance? She had to be at least a furlong ahead. Could she hold her place for the finish?

Lady M raced toward the final turn, maintaining her strong lead. Gladdie could hardly believe her eyes when the mare thundered past them. After crossing the finish line, Charlie stood up in the stirrups, his arm shooting up in victory. If Gladdie's eyes did not deceive her, the mare had more to give. Remarkable!

Red held the stopwatch out so Gladdie could see the final time, the corners of his mouth curving up. "One minute and fifty-eight seconds flat."

"I concur." Nathaniel held out his stopwatch for her, too, a broad grin on his face.

Her eyes widened, and her mouth dropped open—and for good reason this time. "Hot tamale! She broke every record we've ever had at Velvet Brooks."

Red, Nathaniel, and Carter nodded as the jockeys let their horses trot toward them to cool down. Pa would've probably asked Mama to break out a bottle of cherry cordial for something this significant. Gladdie could hardly wait to write to them. No, maybe she'd telephone and tell Pa the good news so he could hear the excitement in her voice.

She could never think about giving the horse up to

its mysterious sender now, even if they could figure out who that was. If it had been Clay, she no longer really wanted to know. The mare had tremendous potential if they could train her to duplicate her performance consistently.

"Well done, Lady M," she whispered under her breath. "Well done."

A horse like that could help her save the farm.

CHAPTER NINE

Be careful for nothing, but in everything by prayer and
supplication with thanksgiving let your requests be
made known to God. And the peace of God, which
passeth all understanding, shall keep your hearts and
minds through Christ Jesus.
—Philippians 4:6-7, KJV

Lottie Belle

Jake Williams, Delia's husband, shook his head,
clearly trying extra hard not to chuckle after
inspecting the crunched front end of the Roadster
parked near his porch. He stood back and scratched
behind his ear. "Let me get this straight. Your sister
drove your beautiful motor carriage into my sister-in-

law's fence, wrecking the fence, your rented motor carriage, and quite possibly, your already fragile chances with Gladdie. Is that right?"

Clay heaved a sigh and nodded. "That about sums it up." He glanced up at the third-floor window of Callie's bedroom, thankful she was currently unpacking upstairs while simultaneously entertaining the children. She provided a much-needed and pleasant distraction for them, but it wouldn't be long before they'd come dashing out the front door to ask about the wagon ride, if Jake might oblige him with a ride to town. He needed lumber, and right quick.

Jake let out a low whistle and shook his head again. "I'm so sorry. I know you said you were hoping to win her back and all."

Clay raked a hand through his hair. It didn't look good, but the way he figured, he at least had a reason to talk to Gladdie again. Maybe *after* he completed the repairs rather than before. No, maybe before. Bother if he knew which might be better. Gladdie was about as unpredictable as a skittish horse at present.

Jake's mouth twisted, and his forehead creased into a few wrinkles. "She's probably gonna show up here makin' a fuss if you don't get to fixin' her fence right away. The Lyndon ladies can be a force to reckon with."

"And don't I know it." It surprised him some that she hadn't come out of the farmhouse already with a shotgun.

Jake bent to have another look at the motor under

the deformed, open hood. "I don't know. We may need to tie a rope to your machine and haul it behind a wagon into town to be repaired. Not sure if she'll make it that far on her own."

Clay crossed his arms over his chest. "I think that's a fair estimation. Do you happen to know where I can purchase some lumber in town to fix the fence? And would you mind if I borrow your wagon and a team, or could you give me a ride?"

Jake stood up straight. "Tell you what. I've got some boards in the barn because I'm getting ready to fence in more of our property. I'll just add them to next month's balance and pick up some more boards next time I'm in Lexington. And you can borrow the wagon and team to take them across Cornflower Road to make the repairs. You'll have to go into town to the hardware store for paint, though."

"Oh, wow." Clay brightened, standing up taller. Delia's husband would save him hours of aggravation. How could he ever thank the man? "That would be amazing." He'd add some extra funds to whatever the lumber would cost.

"And whenever you're ready, we can try pulling your automobile into the livery. I assume you rented it there."

"That would be right fine, Jake. For now, I'll get to work fixin' that fence."

"Follow me. I'll help you hitch up the team." Jake gestured and started across the yard. "You'll need some tools too. Do you want a hand with the fence?"

"Might not be a bad idea if you don't mind…and thank you." He heaved a sigh and whispered another of those prayers toward heaven, following Jake to the barn.

What was that Scripture he'd read last night? *All things work together for good to them that love God, to them who are the called according to his purpose.* If he was called to marry Gladdie, and seeing how his love for the Lord had begun to mend, maybe God had a plan in allowing this to happen.

Funny how he'd found himself drawn to reading the Bible again after seeing how faithful Delia and Jake were in their reading of the Word. He had a lot of catching up to do, but some of the Scriptures were coming back already. He shouldn't have let the rough patches in life turn him into a fair-weather friend to God. He needed to be loyal, but could he truly maintain his newfound determination to be faithful to the Lord if He didn't answer his prayers where Gladdie was concerned?

Later that morning, Clay heaved a sigh before jumping down from the wagon Jake had parked in front of Velvet Brooks. Jake waited in the driver's seat. Clay needed to tell Gladdie about the damage he'd caused and that he had come to repair the fence. But when he reached the front door of Velvet Brooks, he couldn't bring himself to lift the knocker.

He gulped and raked a hand through his hair before returning his hat to his head. He'd abandoned his suit and borrowed a pair of dungarees from Jake.

Jake stopped whistling. "Want me to help you tell her?"

Clay turned to face the wagon. "Might not be a bad idea..."

Exuberant voices headed toward the veranda from the direction of the horse barn.

"Ah, here she comes now." Jake wrapped the reins around the parking gear and climbed down.

Clay's eyes locked with Gladdie's for a moment as she headed toward them with the Velvet Brooks groom, rendering him speechless. Her smile disappeared at the sight of him, and she stopped talking. What he wouldn't give to kiss her just one more time...to return a smile to her face.

"Hey there, Jake, Clay." When Carter—if Clay remembered his name right— and Gladdie reached them, the groom tipped his hat in their direction. "Long time, no see."

Clay could only nod, but it was nice that Carter had remembered and recognized him. Once he told her what had happened, would Gladdie start hollering at him? Kick him off the property? And he had to remember not to blame his sister. The less said about that, the better.

"Gentlemen." Gladdie looked between them as Clay

sidled up to stand beside Jake. Maybe her brother-in-law's presence would help keep Gladdie calm.

May as well dive in. "Um, we've had a...well...a little run in." Why couldn't he find the words?

She crossed her arms, waiting, one brow arched as she tilted her head.

Jake put a hand on his shoulder. "What Clay here is trying to say is that we're about to fix the fence his motor carriage broke."

Clay nodded, finding his tongue. "That about sums it up." And phew! Jake had said it perfectly.

Jake continued, wisely changing the subject. "You two looked happy just now. What's happened?"

Gladdie's wide and beautiful smile returned, and her chocolate-colored eyes lit up. "Lady M just broke the record for any horse we've ever had."

"Lady who?" Clay raised one eyebrow.

"Lady M for *mystery*." Carter grinned.

Jake clapped his hands together. "That's wonderful news! Have you told your father yet?"

Clay smiled too. This must be the filly he'd sent her from New York. He liked the name they'd given her. So she hadn't guessed yet. He could hardly wait to tell her the truth, but he still had to earn her trust and friendship all over again. One step at a time.

"I'm on my way to telephone Pa now," Gladdie informed them, crossing her arms over her chest. "As for the broken fence, I expect you'll let me know when it's mended, and try not to do any other damage to our beautiful farm with that modern menace to society."

Her frosty tone was laced with irritation and grumpiness. So she wanted to take it that way, did she? He crossed his arms over his chest, too, mimicking her. "Speaking of modern menaces, Velvet Brooks has a telephone? How'd you talk your pa into that?"

Gladdie tapped a foot and glared at him. "It was all his doing. How else would Pa check up on us from the ocean?"

"Best we get crackin' before the day gets away from us." Jake elbowed him and then climbed back up to the wagon seat.

Jake's good sense probably spared him from agitating Gladdie any further than he had. She sure did seem annoyed with him. He walked around the front of the team and climbed up into the passenger side of the wagon seat before offering a friendly wink at Gladdie.

No smile in return. She only shook her head and stared after them briefly before heading inside. The wagon rumbled away from the veranda, and Jake steered them across the front lawn to the broken fence.

Clay turned toward Jake. "Thanks for saving the day."

"You're welcome. All in all, she took it pretty well, but if looks could talk, I'd say she's none too pleased."

"I reckon you're right, which is why I plan on buying some more paint to help her finish painting all this fencing." He waved toward the left side of the property where most of the fences meandered.

"Not a bad idea. I've been hoping to get caught up with my work at Lottie Belle to help her, but with the spring plowing and getting our kitchen garden going, I'm barely keeping up. But we can head to town after we have the fence mended to get the paint at the hardware store. We'll need some of it for this section."

"Good plan. I know two or three little ones who'd like a ride in the wagon when we go." Clay nodded toward the Victorian house atop the crest at Lottie Belle.

"Whoa!" Jake pulled the reins in as he parked the wagon and applied the brake. "Sure. If we hurry, we can pick up the girls from school too. I bet they'd all enjoy a ride."

Clay sighed, thankful. The Lord had prepared Jake with the wagon and lumber he needed, and sent the man along to help smooth his way. Maybe, if he worked hard to help Gladdie paint those fences, she would see that he meant everything he said, and she'd tear down the fence in her heart standing between them.

CHAPTER TEN

Take therefore no thought for the morrow; for the morrow shall take thought for the things of itself. Sufficient unto the day is the evil thereof.
—Matthew 6:34, KJV

MARCH 7, 1908
VELVET BROOKS

"No, Clay, there is no need for you to help me paint anything else. You've repaired the fence." Gladdie glanced at the timepiece pinned to the white shirtwaist tucked into her serviceable black skirt. "And you've completed the repairs before six o'clock on the same day as the regrettable incident. That is all that was necessary."

She resumed painting the board in front of her. Sure, some part of her would love to have help with painting the fencing. The staff at Velvet Brooks were busy with other tasks, but she couldn't bring herself to accept aid from him. And though she wanted to know who the lady was who had driven the motor carriage into it in the first place, she had refused to make such an inquiry. The men in the barn were curious about it too. At some point soon, she'd see Delia. Then maybe this mystery would also be resolved.

"No, I want to help." Clay gestured to Jake's wagon across the yard. "I've already gone to town and purchased extra paint at the hardware store. I brought my own brushes, and I won't take no for an answer. It's the very least I can do. You have miles of fencing here. You need some help. And besides, I need to earn my trust with you again somehow."

Earn her trust? Indeed! But if he kept talking like this, and being so nice, how could she keep saying no to him? Besides, the spring rains would start again soon enough, and she couldn't waste a moment if she wanted to finish her task before Pa returned. Not that she knew yet how she would purchase enough paint if she didn't accept his offer of assistance and the supply he'd brought her. Perhaps in autumn, if Lady M won enough races, they could paint the whole farmhouse.

Not knowing how to respond to his statement, she reached for the container of paint and moved with her paintbrush to the next few feet of the board. At least she hadn't bumped into the fence today, but if Clay kept pestering her, she'd surely end up doing so. She'd worn another pinafore-style work apron, one of her oldest ones, and pinned her hair up, but splotches of paint covered her hands.

He'd stood so close as she'd worked on the last section of fence, following her every step of the way, trying to convince her to let him paint. His intoxicatingly wonderful cologne had tickled her nose, his muscles flexing on his tanned forearms visible since he'd rolled his sleeves up. And why did she swoon a little at the sight of his broad shoulders filling out his crisp white shirt so nicely? He certainly wasn't the lanky, thin teenager he'd been at nineteen! Though he'd been plenty handsome then too.

Drat! He followed her again, not one to give up so easily. Yet inside, in an utter paradox of emotions, she was also cheering. Was there hope for the two of them, after all? And when had she begun to allow hope to rise?

Her mind continued to swirl with moments of agitation about the identity of the woman driving the motor carriage. Her younger self would have found a reason to visit Lottie Belle and ask her sister if she knew. Delia and Jake had a telephone, and she'd even thought about placing a call to inquire, but what if Clay overheard her questioning Delia?

"I can't put all of the paint I purchased to waste. I brought extra in case you can use some. There's an awful lot here still left to paint. I'm going to start over there." He pointed to a large section of corral that she hadn't gotten to yet, behind the horse barn. "I'll let you know how I'm doing from time to time. And to save you the hassle of going to town for more paint, I'll leave the paint supply in the horse barn. Help yourself whenever you need it."

She squinted under the brim of her straw hat in the direction he pointed as she considered how she might turn him down. She'd planned to save that section for last, but she could see it was futile to argue with him. She also couldn't argue that his paint might not match, not with a perfectly matched repair completed along the road.

He'd purchased paint, after all. And she'd worried all afternoon about how she would afford to finish the project. In fact, she only had enough paint left to complete the day's work and maybe for a few more sections in the coming days, but he didn't need to know that.

She needn't be so prideful as to turn him down when the Lord had provided, even if He had used Clay to do so. As Mama said, God worked in mysterious ways.

Sighing, she shrugged, barely looking at him as she slathered more paint on her brush. Her muscles ached, and she was too weary and dizzy from bending to reach the bottom rails to argue. "Suit yourself. Mind you alert the men so they don't turn the horses out to pasture with wet paint on the inside of the corral."

"Will do. I'm off to take supplies to the barn. See you around…"

Before she could find another objection, he disappeared toward his wagon. She frowned. If she could come up with a good reason, she probably would send him away—except she couldn't find any, and he was slowly wearing down all of her defenses. He'd found a way to blend in at the farm.

Maybe Delia was right. He seemed awfully determined to win her back. He hadn't spent any time today with the lady who'd crashed into her fence.

She followed his progress toward the wagon with her eyes, somewhat amazed at how the Lord had worked her problems out. Truth be told, if she had the funds, she'd likely have hired someone to handle the monumental painting task. She may as well accept Clay's offer, although it irritated and humbled her to do so.

There was also something oddly comforting about having a man around who refused to forget she existed, even though she'd requested it.

MARCH 11, 1908

On a Wednesday evening four days later, Gladdie stood back from the fencing between the horse barn and the carriage house, taking in all their work, but particularly the section she'd just finished. Satisfied with the second coat on the final section left to paint, she couldn't help but marvel at how the weather had cooperated and how fast the work had gone with Clay's help.

Shading her eyes from the sunshine, she tried to assess his progress on the enclosure beyond the carriage house. A cold breeze made her shiver, even in the sun, warning her it might rain on Thursday. He'd finished the series of corrals behind the horse barn, and now she'd finished everything in the front along the road, near the horse barn, and near the house.

They'd painted the rails along the racetrack, too, him working the outside rail while she completed the inside rail. Not close enough for any conversation, but the silence suited her, for now. She had to admit, she enjoyed the moments when he'd approached her to take a break or when he smiled at her. Martin had brought them lemonade a few times too. Sometimes one of the staff in the barn came outside to talk, mostly with Clay instead of her. But she'd noticed he kept working despite the interruptions.

For most of three whole days, he had become a fixture at Velvet Brooks. She hadn't seen him at church on Sunday, but the day had been rainy and cold. Lots of folks had stayed home.

Should she thank him? Mama would have thanked him. They'd made light work of the enormous project. Pa would be pleased.

Two little voices and laughter in the distance caused her to spin around. No, not Delia and Jake's children. Clay's children? Grace had mentioned two children, and curiosity surged through Gladdie.

She set her paint and brush aside as the two little figures headed toward the creek on the eastern edge of the property. They were awfully young. How had they escaped from Lottie Belle unattended? The creek was usually quite high this time of year. Did they know how to swim?

Gladdie set off across the property at a trot. When she caught up to them, she noticed the little boy had a toy sailboat tucked under an arm, and the little girl carried a doll.

"Ho, there!" she called out, waving as they turned, a friendly smile on her face.

They waited for her, eyes wide, likely unsure of what to expect.

Breathless from chasing them across the lawn, she managed an introduction when she caught up to them. "Hello, I'm Gladdie. I live here. What are your names?"

The older girl held the hem of her dress with one hand, her doll in the other. "I'm Ollie, and this is Emery, my brother."

Ollie? How unusual a name for a girl. She didn't appear much like Clay, and with her brown curls and brown eyes, she didn't resemble Alice either. In fact, she looked more like...Gladdie herself. "Nice to meet you, Emery and Ollie. Is Ollie your nickname?"

Ollie nodded with her brown eyes wide, brown curls bouncing, and her expression quite serious. "My name is Olympia, and I'm a'sposed to use it whenever I meet strangers."

Gladdie smiled. How odd to meet Clay's children without him. "That's quite a strong name."

More nodding and curls bouncing. "Father says so too. Sometimes he calls me Olive."

"Ah, a very sweet nickname as well." The monikers made her smile.

"We're going to sail my boat in the creek. We've already tried it in the pond." Emery held up his sailboat, somehow making his sailor suit all the more adorable.

"I see. Do you know how to swim?" Gladdie knelt to the ground, patting it to entice them to sit. She had to distract them from the creek and come up with a way to return them to Lottie Belle or else find Clay.

"I do, but Emery is still learning. We've had swimming lessons with Father," Ollie informed her, tilting her chin up as she sat where Gladdie indicated and spread her pretty dress out while clutching her doll. Her brother followed suit, placing his sailboat before him. Everything about these children bespoke money and lots of it. From the wide ribbon atop Ollie's head to the elaborate sailboat and their shiny new shoes, their possessions appeared detailed and costly.

"Well, you know, one should never be around a fast-running, deep creek, or really any amount of water without one's nanny or parents. Did you know that?" She'd crashed their bubble of hope about sailing Emery's boat in the creek. Their sad little faces tugged on her heart. "You should ask your pa first, for safety reasons."

"There you are, children. Miss Lyndon is right. You should always ask your pa first before doing anything." Clay's voice from behind startled them, his long strides catching up to where they sat on the lawn.

Ollie sat up straighter at her father's presence. "Pa, is this the Miss Lyndon who is going to the ball with you?"

Gladdie resisted the urge to giggle as she glanced up at Clay's face, which was frozen with his eyes wide and brows raised. No doubt, he struggled to find the right answer. Turning back to the little girl she judged to be about six years old, she nodded. What better way to let Clay know she had appreciated his help and would give him a chance? "Yes, I'm the Miss Lyndon he is escorting to the ball. Now that we've finished painting miles of fencing..." A spontaneous decision, the admission somehow seemed right. He had worked hard to prove himself trustworthy to her. And while he still had a long way to go in that regard, perhaps this was a step in the right direction for them.

Ollie clasped her hands together. "Will you wear a pretty dress like a princess?"

She smiled, trying to steal another surreptitious glance at Clay's reaction. "I do hope I resemble a princess for the ball, but yes, a very pretty dress in a shade of periwinkle. And I imagine your pa will wear a cutaway dinner jacket, maybe with black pants. And likely a white collared shirt, a white vest, white tie or cravat, and kid gloves of white or some other pale hue." Clay undoubtedly knew all of this from being married to a debutante like Alice, who would have insisted he escort her to the best events society had to offer. But it was never too early to teach the children about proper etiquette when occasion gave opportunity.

Clay sat down beside her on the lawn, placing a hand over hers, their eyes locking on each other's for one moment. Had she been transported to some other land where no problems had ever existed between them?

"Oh my." The enraptured sigh drew Gladdie's attention. Ollie smiled, her eyes shining, her face alight with a dreamy expression.

Another peek at Clay revealed the corners of his mouth turned up in a smile with his blue eyes dancing. Perhaps he imagined them twirling as one in each other's arms around the Sullivan ballroom? Had her acceptance of his invitation rendered him speechless?

"I can't wait until I'm old enough to go to a ball. I can dress like a princess, and Pa will buy me a tiara, and

Emery can dress like a prince. Right, Emery?" Ollie elbowed her younger brother.

Emery jumped to his feet and pretended to draw an imaginary sword from an imaginary sheath. "I will be Prince Emery, and you shall be Princess 'Lympia."

A lady wrapped in a shawl ran toward them, breathless, stopping some feet away. She cupped her hands over her mouth and called out, "Yoohoo! Children! Where have you been? I lost you. What a scare you've given your auntie."

Callie Grinstead? Gladdie hadn't seen Clay's sister in nearly a decade. She'd put on a few pounds. No wonder Gladdie hadn't recognized her before, but now she knew who'd driven his motor carriage into their fence. She and Callie, and Cora for a time, had attended Lexington's Finishing School for Ladies when they were about fifteen, sixteen, and seventeen years old. His sisters had earned scholarships to attend, but then Cora had been whisked away into that dreadful place, and Callie...she had disappeared shortly after Clay had married Alice Parker. Why did it seem a lifetime ago?

Clay cleared his throat. "Children, go with Aunt Callie and wash up for dinner while I have a private word with Miss Lyndon. I'll be home in a few minutes."

"Yes, Pa! Prince Emery shall lead the way." Emery scooped up his sailboat. He saluted his father, raised his pretend sword in a charge, and took off toward his aunt.

Ollie scrambled to her feet, rushed into Clay's arms

to kiss his cheek, and then, turning, called out, "Wait for Princess Olympia!"

They watched the children run to Callie, who waved toward them before leading her charges across Cornflower Road, a child holding onto both of her hands.

Gladdie broke the silence between them first. "They are lovely, Clay."

He offered a weak smile, but his brows furrowed. "Most of the time. I'll be having a stern discussion with all three of them after dinner this evening. They shouldn't have escaped with a plan to sail their boat in the creek, and where was Callie when all this happened? But enough about that." He turned toward her, placing a finger under her chin, leaning forward, and brushing her lips with a tender kiss.

Even after he withdrew his lips, her heart melted. All of it. How good it felt to be kissed by her one true love. But when had she begun to think of him as *that* man again?

"Did you mean it? Will you permit me to escort you to the ball?" His blue eyes searching hers, his voice sounded low, barely above a whisper.

She nodded and looked down, breaking away from his touch, thankful her lashes concealed her eyes since she must now navigate a complicated answer. "Yes, I did mean it. I don't know why, except I can see you will only persist in wearing down every excuse I might find. And I *have* already purchased a ball gown for the occasion. And somehow, against my better judgement, you have convinced me to give us a second chance. So, yes, I'll permit you to escort me to the ball, but I am taking this slowly, Clay Grinstead."

"I understand." His response pulsated with barely restrained joy.

She flashed him a quick look, a bit chidingly. "I'm not entirely convinced it's the right thing to do, all things considered. You must know I hold a great many reservations, and I cannot say you have fully earned my trust yet."

"I understand." The same two words, more firmly.

Gladdie pressed her lips together. "That said, you may pick me up at seven o'clock sharp for the ball. And if you like, bring a wrist corsage from the florist. Something in white or pink would make a nice contrast with my gown."

He tilted her chin toward him again and locked his gaze on hers. "You won't regret it, Gladiola. I've thought of nothing but you since long before I left New York, and I have so much I want to offer you. You'll see. I will make up for everything, every tear, every sorrow...if it's how I spend every minute for the rest of my life."

He had rendered her speechless with his sincerity. But could she trust him this time? Did he genuinely mean what he said, or was it all sweet talk?

A gentle breeze blew across the lawn, causing wisps of her hair to disobey framing her face. He reached out to tuck a strand behind her ear.

"It *was* you." The tenderness in his expression, his

promises to do anything necessary to woo her, made her suddenly certain. "*You* sent Lady M to me on Valentine's Day."

Clay's eyes lit up, and he smiled, extending a hand to help her to her feet as he rose. "Do you like the mare?"

A smile played on her lips. "I'd be telling you a lie if I said I didn't."

His smile reflected genuine warmth, warmth which reached his eyes. "Good. I'm very glad. She belongs here at Velvet Brooks. Say you'll marry me. It can be as long or as short an engagement as you desire, but the biggest wedding Lexington has ever seen."

She winced, more from the pain of bending over for days on end to reach railings with her paint brush than the remedy he spoke of for the broken part of her heart. "It's much too soon for that, Clay. Go home and have dinner with your children. Soak in a hot bath. Get some rest. It's been a long day. We are both tired, sore, and hungry from all of this painting..."

He nodded, hanging his head. "I know it's too soon, but I want to make clear to you my intentions. I don't want to leave you wondering where we are going for one more hour or one more day. I promise you a proper courtship, if you want one."

She arched her eyebrow. "One day at a time, for right now." The pangs of her aching muscles wouldn't let her consider anything beyond the ball, for now. And she needed time to contemplate all he'd said. She had to hold some part of her heart back until she could be sure about everything, but his declaration caused her heart to beat faster. "Thank you for your help with all of the painting."

"You are welcome." He pulled one of her hands to his lips and brushed it with an affectionate and solemn kiss. "See you soon."

"See you soon." She turned toward the farmhouse, the feel of his kisses on her hand and lips a pleasant distraction to warm her heart and soften her cool demeanor with him.

Was her heart beating extra hard as she crossed the lawn, heading for the main house? Of course, it was. Their first kiss had left her swooning. But she mustn't let it all carry her too far, too fast. She must guard her heart and pray for wisdom.

At least two mysteries were now solved. His sister had driven the automobile into her fence, and he'd sent Lady M to her.

Could she keep this extravagant gift from Clay? He certainly wanted her to.

No, she couldn't return Lady M, not when the filly had a chance of winning so many races, beginning with the upcoming Phoenix Stakes on the Lexington Association Track—Gladdie's only hope in saving Velvet Brooks from ruin at this point.

But would Clay prove to be faithful and trustworthy if she gave him her heart this time? Dare she take a second chance on him?

Reaching the house, she paused to pluck a bloom and smiled at the trumpet lily in her hands, its lemon scent wafting under her nose as she breathed in. Pa always called them moon lilies because they opened their petals in the evenings, blooming in adversity. So much like herself. And her relationship with Clay. Moon Lily. Yes, that was it...the official name she would give Lady M now that the mystery had been solved.

But the mystery of what had happened when Clay had abandoned her that night so long ago still troubled her. Perhaps it was time to finally ask him.

CHAPTER ELEVEN

For God hath not given us the spirit of fear, but of
power, and of love, and of a sound mind.
—2 Timothy 1:7

MARCH 16, 1908
VELVET BROOKS

The next morning, Gladdie followed Mr. James Blount from his carriage to the horse barn, practically skipping to keep up with the man. In her leather riding boots, jodhpurs, and tweed jacket instead of her riding habit, at least she could look the part of a savvy businesswoman. But unfortunately, she had no idea why he'd come to retrieve his horse, other than his complaining he could no longer afford their training services. Mr. Blount's Gibraltar was their best—and very last—steed to be boarded and trained, other than Jake's horse, sired by Horizon, so she needed to keep the man happy.

"But Mr. Blount, I'm sure we can work something out for you." *Think, Gladdie, think! Negotiate with the man. Offer him a deal he can't refuse...*

"I'm sorry, Miss Lyndon. But haven't you heard the news?"

"The news?" She blinked. Drat! She hadn't had breakfast yet, when she generally glanced through the headlines over a cup of tea or coffee and a plate of scrambled eggs after her morning horseback excursion. She didn't prefer to go riding on a full stomach, and he'd come awfully early.

"Yes. You *do* read the newspaper in your father's absence, don't you?" Mr. Blount marched on as if reaching the stall housing his beautiful bay was a matter of life or death.

"Yes, I do read the paper, *after* my morning ride. Our horses and their exercise come first at Velvet Brooks. And your horse, Gibraltar—he loves his morning exercise." She needn't mention that Hank had assigned Gibraltar's morning ride to Charlie Ford, but she knew Charlie rode him even before Moon Lily. "If you're referring to the news that New York legislators have introduced a bill to put an end to horseracing in their state, I am already aware. It hasn't happened yet. It will take years before they can pass a law of that kind, if they can pass it all. We can still look forward to the seaside races at Coney Island. Gibraltar did so well there last year, Mr. Blount. And we do still have the Phoenix Stakes and the Derby in Kentucky. Latonia is still open, too, and Pimlico for the Preakness, and at least a dozen other possibilities throughout the country..."

"You'd be wise to read today's paper, Miss Lyndon. And in view of that, I am hereby terminating my agreement for services. You'll understand...when you read the newspaper." He trudged on, casting a glance in her direction as if he harbored doubts she actually read the papers.

She skipped to keep up. "But Mr. Blount, you have been with us for as long as I can remember." He had renewed his contract each year since the age she could only ride a pony. Why, he had been as permanent a fixture as the horse barn itself. "I'm sure Pa is counting on retaining your services while he is away. And quite frankly, we need your business..." If he withdrew his horse from training with Red Brickman, their highly successful trainer, horseracing must be in a great deal more trouble than she had suspected. And what could she do to fix any of it?

He turned into the barn and strode toward his stallion's stall, ignoring her plea. Reaching it, he opened the door, and taking hold of both leather straps in one swipe, he led Gibraltar out of the stall.

Gladdie bit her lower lip, refraining from reminding him that the current lead on the horse belonged to

Velvet Brooks. She may as well let him have it as a souvenir. A piece of the farm's history was literally walking away, and there was nothing she could say or do to stop it as Hank, Carter, and Nathaniel stared on at the scene in silence. At least Red wasn't there. She could break the news to him gently, later.

"As I said, I've left a bank draft with Martin up at the house for the balance of what I owe you. You'll not see a penny more." The client shook a pudgy finger at her and then turned on his heel, marching out of the barn, Gibraltar's clopping echoing on the cement floor.

Gladdie gave up trying to keep pace with the stubborn man—let alone trying to convince him to stay. She crossed her arms over her chest, lingering near the empty stall. The time had come to face the facts. Her efforts to save Velvet Brooks had failed. One by one, their last few training clients had left. Pa would be so disappointed in her, but she'd done her best under the circumstances.

Why couldn't she think of some way to save their clients? Surely, she could come up with something if she prayed hard enough. The men in the barn were counting on her—not to mention their jockeys, the household staff, and her family. She'd figure something out, but what? Perhaps when she had a better handle on her emotions, she could speak to Hank. As the farm's manager, surely, he would have some ideas.

Her hands balled into tight fists, she stomped out of the barn before Hank or anyone else could discover her with misty eyes. Blinking back the tears as she headed toward the house, she could see Mr. Blount had already tied his champion stallion to the rear of his carriage and now steered toward the lane.

She whispered a prayer. "Lord, please help me. You promised You wouldn't forsake me. You asked me to have courage. I'm counting on You."

Drinking from the well of deep and abiding trust in her Savior, she fought down a variety of emotions tugging at her heart, soul, and mind.

Well, she trusted Him except for maybe where it came to her broken heart because of Clay. She hadn't been able to figure out what the Lord was doing there, but it kind of felt as if He was preparing her for something bigger by crushing every possible evil from her soul. A purging, if you will. A humbling of sorts.

Surely, the Lord wouldn't leave them now. He'd always brought her through every trouble, though sometimes it didn't work out the way she thought it should. He'd get her through this too.

Swiping tears away, she stepped onto the veranda. Time for a cup of hot coffee and a look at the day's headlines. She'd already worked up an appetite, but why did her stomach seem a bundle of knots?

This was no time to cry. She had to be strong for all of them. Obviously, Harvey or someone else at the *Lexington Gazette* had written something to scare away her last client. He wouldn't do it on purpose. He was only doing his job, reporting the news as assigned to him by his boss.

If she were a man, she could attend the Lexington Jockey Club meetings and understand more about what should be done.

Once Gladdie was seated at the breakfast table, Martin slid a cup of coffee in front of her. He handed her a steaming plate of scrambled eggs with two slices of bacon and one of Willamena's fluffy biscuits. He offered a folded copy of the *Gazette*, simultaneously placing a dish of blackberry preserves within reach.

"Thank you, Martin."

"Can I get you anything else?"

She shook her head, taking note of the sugar, creamer, and butter dishes at her fingertips. "No, but thank you. Everything looks delicious." She added cream and sugar to the coffee, tasted a few bites after bowing her head in prayer, and unfolded the newspaper.

The headline, all in caps, stared back at her. PHOENIX STAKES CANCELED BY COURT ORDER. Her mouth dropped open. In smaller letters, she read, *by Harvey Higginbottom.*

Oh, Harvey! Must you do your job so efficiently?

No wonder Mr. Blount had retrieved his horse. If Gibraltar couldn't participate in the races, why bother paying to train him? Especially since dozens of other racecourses around the country had also closed in recent months. If she'd seen this coming, she might have been able to assure her clients they could set up racing campaigns on tracks remaining open, but she had *not* seen this coming. And who could tell which track would shut down next, with new closings happening almost every other month?

The article went on to say that a group of individuals against the greedy bookmakers had applied in court for an injunction to stop the race, presenting a petition signed by thousands of individuals with an anti-betting sentiment. The judge had granted their request.

Would the same thing happen to the Kentucky Derby and the Latonia track near Cincinnati? If so, Moon Lily would have nowhere to race locally, but the mare deserved every chance to prove herself on the track. With Velvet Brooks hanging on by a thread, what was Gladdie going to do?

After breakfast, she turned her attention toward another matter that had been pressing on her heart since Mary's birthday party—penning a letter to Clay. She intended to give him the letter after the ball if he couldn't answer one question in particular to her satisfaction. What had happened that night seven years ago to change his mind about meeting her at the train and going on to Richmond to marry her?

It was doubtful anything he could say would build enough trust to repair the damage. Wouldn't he have said something more in the sitting room if he'd had good reason to marry Alice? To be fair, though, she wasn't sure if she'd given him much of a chance to speak freely that first time he had called upon her. Nor had she clearly asked about his reasons for what he'd done. In fact, she hadn't been ready to listen to any of his reasons. But now she was.

Though she hadn't seen him interact much with Miss Aurelia Jacobs at Mary's birthday party, the idea of him falling in love with some other lady terrified her. And now, Miss Jacobs had all but moved into Lottie Belle, where she could captivate him every morning and each evening to her heart's content.

No, Gladdie needed a man she could rely upon. Though he had worked hard around her farm, it hadn't been enough to prove his trustworthiness. Her heart could not survive another break, nor could she see herself living a life of looking over her shoulder, continually questioning Clay's loyalty.

What if he danced with any number of debutantes at the ball? Surely, they would flock around him, given the rumors circulating about his new wealth. She did not look forward to this possibility.

She would do her best to enjoy the ball with him, after which she'd give him a chance to answer her question in private. Then she must be ready to decline him, depending on his response and his demeanor at the ball.

While her parents might urge her to consider him because of his wealth, and particularly now, since uniting with him could save Velvet Brooks, she refused to marry him for anything other than love.

She reached for a pen and began writing.

Dear Clay,

I'm writing to tell you the reasons why we can never marry...which can all be summarized in one statement. I cannot survive another heartbreaking situation. Therefore, after much prayer and consideration, I regret to inform you that I cannot marry you or continue to carry on a romantic relationship with you. I pray you will find happiness and peace in marital bliss one day...but all we can ever be is good friends.

Sincerely,

Gladdie

When the ink had dried, she folded the letter. Opening the clasp to the faux-pearl-covered handbag she intended to carry on the evening of the ball, she tucked it inside. Would he respect her wishes this time if he saw her request in writing?

And if he surprised her with his answer, she could easily change her mind about giving him the note. Did she dare to hope?

CHAPTER TWELVE

Looking forward to things is half the pleasure of them.
—L. M. Montgomery

MARCH 17, 1908
VELVET BROOKS

The evening of the ball finally arrived. The whole world seemed abuzz with excitement. Grace set about styling Gladdie's hair in an elaborate updo with pearl-edged combs and extra hairpins to hold everything in place. Since Mama had taken Frances, Gladdie's customary maid, to Chesapeake Manor, Gladdie now had a superior stylist for the evening with Grace tending to her needs.

Gladdie tried to sit perfectly still while the maid

worked her wonders. Grace held curling tongs over a gas burner. Then, after winding a long lock of Gladdie's hair around and around on the hot iron, she clamped the tongs closed.

A few seconds passed while they waited. After releasing and arranging the curl, Grace stood back and smiled. They stared at Gladdie's reflection in the vanity mirror. "How do you like that?"

"It's lovely. Thank you. I barely recognize myself." The cascade of curls dangling over one shoulder gave her a sophisticated and fashionable appearance. If only she could get through the evening without worrying about their financial troubles or confronting Clay, she'd consider it a success. But deep in her heart, she didn't know if she could dance the night away under the bleak circumstances facing her. Not to mention, her future with Clay hung in the balance.

Grace secured the final decorative comb and dabbed some sort of pomade all over her curls from a jar selling the promise of keeping each hair in its proper place. "There. Time to get you into your ball gown."

After rising, Gladdie stepped into the periwinkle-colored dress with its lower-cut, lace-covered bodice, short and puffy off-the-shoulder sleeves, sparkling embellishments, and demi-train. The gown made a lovely swishing noise as she stepped out into the hall.

Time to see if Clay approved. Would his eyes light up when he saw her?

Grace handed the purse to her. Her excitement

waned as she remembered the letter inside. Why did she care if he did or didn't approve of her appearance at this point? If he couldn't provide her with the answers she deserved, she would finally end the possibility of him breaking her heart for good. One way or another, by the end of the evening, she was determined to either become nothing more than a mere friend to Clay, or she would have the promise of something more.

Slowly, her gown trailing over each step behind her, she descended the staircase to where Clay waited below. Grace joined Willamena and Martin near the front door. Clay's eyes did light up, and that charming smile he wore…it made her a little dizzy.

He whistled, making her laugh. For just a while, she could forget about the importance she'd attached to the evening and her worries about Velvet Brooks. Taking in his appearance, she smiled. He'd be one of the best-dressed men in the ballroom with his impeccable style. He wore a black cutaway, tuxedo-style dinner jacket, and matching suit trousers. His vest looked crisp below the white cravat at the neck of his wing-tipped shirt. Shiny black shoes completed his look, accompanied by the scent of a musky cologne wafting about him as she drew near. His handsome appearance made her sway a little when he slid a pink corsage on her wrist. Was she in a dream?

"You look simply radiant, Gladdie. So beautiful." His blue eyes glowed as he perused her.

"You're looking rather handsome yourself." She

reached up and tucked one of his unruly waves of hair in place, earning an affectionate yet sheepish grin.

"Are you ready for a short carriage ride?" His brow arched as he held his arm toward her.

She nodded, placing her hand on his arm. As she turned, her glance through the screen at the open front door brought a smile to her face when she took in the elaborate black leather crownpieces, ornate brow and nose bands, fancy breast collars, and burnished brass buckles the horses wore. "Ah, I see you've made sure our team is wearing the best of celebration and dressage tack. Another thoughtful touch. My father would be impressed."

Willamena handed an elegant, fringed shawl Gladdie meant to wear to Clay, and he draped it over her shoulders. "Thank you. I think we're ready. Don't wait up late, everyone."

Too bad Pa and Mama weren't here to see them off, but perhaps it was for the best. No need to get their hopes up if nothing of note came of the evening. Grace, Willamena, and Martin crowded the hall enough as it was, all of them looking pleased.

"Have a wonderful time," Grace called when they stepped onto the veranda, the staff clambering out of the house after them. "Mind you don't forget about your train going through doors and climbing into carriages."

"Thank you, and yes, I'll be careful."

Clay helped her up into Jake's open carriage, and after he settled in on the seat beside her, she waved to their onlookers. Carter, dressed in top hat and his finest livery uniform, turned around and tipped his hat in her direction, offering a sly grin from the driver's seat, making her struggle to suppress a giggle.

Then they were off. It would take only a few minutes to reach Sullivan Hill, but by the time she returned, would her life be changed for good?

~

Gladdie took Clay's breath away. She'd be the most beautiful girl in the room with her dazzling evening gown, and he could hardly wait to dance the night away with her in his arms... finally. Before the evening ended, he intended to tell her everything that had happened on that fateful night that had disrupted their plans and changed the course of their lives.

It was time he shared the whole story. Would she understand once she knew the truth? On his first visit to Lottie Belle, Delia had seemed to think that additional information would help. He could only pray that it would be so.

What could he chat about on the short drive? He cleared his throat and turned toward her. "I am curious about what will be on the menu." As Carter turned onto Cornflower Road, Clay caught a glimpse of a long stream of carriages ahead, all going in the same direction of Sullivan Hill.

"Oh, I have a copy of the menu with the invitation right here." Gladdie opened her purse, fished out the invitation, and began reading it. "'Oysters Rockefeller, asparagus toast, and stuffed mushroom caps for hors d'oeuvres. Chilled squash soup and a Waldorf salad for the first course. Roast beef, duck with orange sauce, or ham with mint sauce for the main course. Early spring peas or roasted carrots. Potatoes Julienne and rolls with butter. And for dessert, your choice of orange sponge cake or lemon-flavored Italian ice.'"

"Hmm." He drummed his fingers on some leather trim inside the carriage. "I think I'll try the ham with mint sauce." Why could he think of nothing better to say when all he wanted to do was connect with this amazing woman? Maybe because he could barely look at her, she was so beautiful.

He chanced a glance at her as she tucked the invitation away, mentioning that she might try the beef or duck. "Ollie and Emery are excited about the ball. They want to hear every detail tomorrow at breakfast."

Her face lit up. "I can guess all of the questions they will ask. I remember peeking at Mama when she came downstairs, all dressed up in her finest for attending balls and dinner parties. My sisters and I would lie on the floor and look downstairs through the railings."

He chuckled softly, imagining it. Then he placed his hand over hers. "I only intend to dance with you. Prepare to scandalize the town this evening."

"Oh, Clay…"

But she was smiling and blushing as she looked away. It warmed his heart, and he gave her hand a gentle squeeze. How good it was to see her smiling. He'd give almost anything to convince her to permit him to spend the rest of his life making her happy.

Turning toward him with a raised brow, she tilted her head. "Were you able to secure invitations for your sister and Aurelia? Delia mentioned they had gowns and were excited and hopeful about attending..."

"Yes, as a matter of fact. Caroline Sullivan had someone from their staff deliver them late yesterday morning. They are thrilled, of course. Jabbering all day about it and getting ready. They'll be along with Jake and Delia. There was some problem with Callie's hair, and Aurelia had lost a glove as I was leaving, so they may be running a little behind."

"I'm happy to hear they will be joining us this evening." Gladdie wound a curl that dangled along her shoulder around a finger.

He'd love to kiss the bare skin there...but she would never allow that until they married. And what if she refused him? He mustn't think about that possibility, not tonight. Tonight, he would do everything in his power to ensure she had a wonderful evening at his side.

"It would be nice if a courtship could come out of the evening for my sister. She doesn't get to mingle much with society, living out in the countryside..." Stiffening, he halted what he was about to say. Too close to the subject he would discuss with her later.

Gladdie smiled at him. "And Aurelia? Perhaps I can introduce them to some gentlemen this evening."

He brightened. "I'm sure they would appreciate the gesture."

The stately Sullivan mansion came into view, giving Clay visions of the future—his own home completed and Gladdie installed as its mistress. Would she want to consult on the landscaping and laying out the formal garden?

Carter finally turned onto the drive. Clay gulped and attempted to loosen his cravat a smidgen. Would he fit in with all of these fancy folks and remember the rules of etiquette? The Sullivans would serve him dinner with one too many forks, expect him to ask several ladies to dance, and he needed to remember to greet all the right people.

If only he could devote his attention solely to Gladdie. But that time was coming soon. So much hung in the balance tonight...

Liveried staff held doors open for Clay and Gladdie at the main entrance of Sullivan Hill. Gladdie waited while a male servant took Clay's top hat, placing it in a large cloak room and handing him a numbered ticket so he could retrieve it later. They followed a long line of other guests up a grand staircase to the elegant ballroom on the second floor.

They would have a short wait in the line to greet their hosts since several couples were ahead of them, monopolizing Harold and Caroline Sullivan's time. The couple's five grown children and spouses or dance partners stood alongside them. Gladdie returned a wave to their youngest daughter, her friend Mary Louise Sullivan.

Chandeliers in the ballroom to their left provided soft lighting, potted palms spread their green leaves, and happy guests dressed in their finest mingled or danced as musicians played classical melodies. Uniformed waiters circulated with trays of appetizers and glasses of punch. Eager young gentlemen asked pretty ladies to dance, and others stood back to observe or converse in small groups.

She returned a wave to her Spencer and Lyndon grandparents along the opposite side of the room, nudging Clay, who also waved and nodded. They patted empty chairs beside them, indicating they'd saved them seats. Delia and Jake were probably in line somewhere behind them with Aurelia and Callie by now. Would the vivacious redhead tempt Clay to dance with her?

While it was nice to see Harvey there, taking photographs with his new camera—probably to turn into the *Lexington Gazette* with an article about the event—Gladdie had no desire to dance with him. She snapped open her fan and waved it for some relief from the warm room, leaning toward Clay, keeping her voice low and the fan over her face for some degree of privacy. "Goodness, everyone is here this evening. The Picketts, the Harpers, Gebharts, and the Breckenridges." The friends of her parents were longtime members of the Lexington Jockey Club. "And look, there is Colonel Winn, the one shaking hands with my grandfather, Colonel Lyndon."

"Tell me, who is Colonel Winn?" Clay's gaze traveled to where she indicated.

"He is the president of Churchill Downs. I can't wait to hear what he says about all of these tracks being closed." She'd forgotten to ask Clay if he'd learned about the cancellation of the Phoenix Stakes, but no doubt they'd hear plenty on that topic throughout the evening.

And maybe with all the notable families of horse racing represented, together they could come up with a plan on how to save their mutual livelihood. Because more than Gladdie's personal future was at stake right now...

CHAPTER THIRTEEN

I can do all things through Christ which strengtheneth
me.
—Philippians 4:13, KJV

Harold and Caroline Sullivan offered warm smiles as Clay led Gladdie to greet their long-time family friends. Without her eldest sister and parents among the guests, it was up to her and Delia to help make a good impression on their behalf. They exchanged greetings with their hosts, who inquired after Gladdie's father's health, then she and Clay moved along to greet their children.

The rest of the clan swarmed them all at once. Mary Lou stepped out of her place and whispered to Gladdie from behind her fan that she and Clay could expect to find their place cards situated near her and Thomas at dinner, and also at the same table with Colonel Winn and the Breckenridges.

"Thank you, Mary Lou. I'm looking forward to it." Gladdie waved her fan briskly and smiled in return. She could hardly wait to hear what Colonel Winn would have to say about the state of horseracing. Would Moon Lily ever have a chance to prove herself on the track? Would their regional races survive the relentless attempts to shut down the industry?

"Nice to see you two here," Thaddeus offered, clapping Clay on the back. "Are Jake and Delia coming?"

Gladdie's brow arched. How congenial of Thaddeus to ask about her sister and husband. Did he still long for her sister? She still considered him a vile, uncouth rake, but tonight, she would bite her tongue.

Clay shook hands with Thaddeus. "Yes, they'll be along shortly."

"Good. Glad to hear it." Thaddeus grinned.

Henry shook hands with Clay next, but he turned toward Gladdie. "Colonel Winn is here, Gladdie. Won't it be nice to hear what he has to say about how Churchill Downs is weathering the storm?"

"It certainly will." Henry's question was oddly comforting. Perhaps the Sullivans were in a similar panic to herself. Good of them to put on a brave front despite the challenges.

"Do you think there will be a Derby, Gladdie?" Tillie

leaned forward with furrowed brows as she waved her elegant fan. "Mother is worried."

"I certainly hope so." Gladdie squeezed Tillie's free hand. So they *were* concerned. Confirmation that she wasn't alone in the struggle to survive and keep Velvet Brooks afloat.

"Save a dance for me, Gladdie." Percy winked at her.

"Oh dear, I think my card is already full…" She glanced up at Clay. Hadn't he said he preferred to dance every dance with her? Had he meant it?

"Sorry Percy, I'm reserving all of her dances." Clay clapped him on the back while giving Gladdie a rakishly handsome grin.

Percy pouted momentarily, then brightened as he cast a glance at her escort. "I may have to cut in, then."

Thankfully, Clay whisked her toward the hostess table, where Mrs. Stone, a widow, and Gladdie's Spencer aunts, Eliza and Ida, were seated. How nice that they'd found something useful to do.

Aunt Eliza handed Gladdie a dance card, and Aunt Ida offered her a program, both wearing welcoming smiles. "You look stunning, Gladdie." She leaned toward Ida. "Wouldn't our sister be pleased about how our niece is dressed this evening? Our Gladdie is the prettiest girl here."

Aunt Ida nodded, reaching across the table with a wrinkled hand to pat Gladdie's hand. "You both look marvelous. Such a handsome escort too."

Clay chuckled. "Thank you, ladies."

"Thank you, Aunt Eliza, Aunt Ida, Mrs. Stone. You remember Clay Grinstead, don't you?"

He reached across and shook each of their hands.

When she started to move away, Clay stopped her. "Wait. I'd like to fill in your card." He held up a pencil from the hostess table and grinned.

She handed him her card, her brow arched. He wrote his name in giant letters across every line, effectively taking up all of her dances with one signing, making her laugh and shake her head. But inside, she was cheering.

Did he see the tears brimming in her eyes? She fluttered her eyelashes, blinking several times to clear her vision before she turned into a blubbering idiot. Her aunts and grandparents would think it scandalous for her to dance with the same gentleman all evening. So would a great many others who were present, but why did she suddenly not care what any of them thought?

To her, his gesture meant the whole world. He truly didn't intend to dance with anyone else. If there was a waste bin at hand, she would have reached inside her purse, pulled out her letter and torn it up, and chucked it. As it was, she gulped down all sorts of emotions and allowed Clay to lead her through the sea of guests toward their seats.

She could hardly wait for their first dance. So far, the evening had exceeded her expectations, but why did she have a funny feeling in the pit of her stomach?

Perhaps because the night was young…and anything could happen.

~

Pink-and-white star lilies spread down the middle of the long dining tables, a spectacular backdrop for tall white tapers inside hurricane globes with flickering candlelight. The hall adjoined the ballroom on the second floor. In keeping with societal expectations, no one was seated directly beside their spouse or escort. Nonetheless, Gladdie found herself directly across from Clay.

She'd already danced three times with him. Each spin around the floor had been heavenly. Where had he learned to dance so well? He hadn't missed a single step. He'd probably learned with Alice, but she pushed the notion aside for now. They often locked eyes as they engaged in conversation at their end of the table.

Mary Lou's escort, Thomas Grainger, sat to Gladdie's right, and Colonel Winn sat on her left. Also at their table were Clay, Delia, Jake, Mary Lou, the Picketts, the elder Mr. Breckenridge and his wife, Gladdie's Lyndon grandparents, and Mr. Sullivan. Mrs. Sullivan presided over another table to better tend the needs of their guests.

In fact, Mrs. Sullivan had spread most of their family members at other tables. She had, however, ensured Colonel Winn was seated with a great number of folks who were important in the horseracing community. Gladdie counted it an honor to find herself located where she was. Had Mary Lou played a role in making that happen? She'd have to thank her later.

Mrs. Sullivan asked Gladdie's grandfather, the retired Reverend Spencer, to bless the meal. A hush fell on the assembly as he gave thanks for the bounty of food and fellowship. He paused before adding, "Bless your people, Lord."

Gladdie's eyes misted. How they needed the Lord's blessing if they were to survive the perilous times.

When he finished the prayer, conversations resumed, and the clanking of Mrs. Sullivan's finest china, crystal, and silverware began as waiters brought delectable meals to eager guests.

Harvey Higginbottom joined them at their table, quietly setting aside his new camera and taking the remaining empty seat. Oh dear, would he print everything he discovered?

Halfway through the first course, after some polite small talk, Harold Sullivan lifted a spoonful of the chilled squash soup to his lips, but his eyes were trained on Colonel Winn. "Well, what do you think, Matt? Will there be a Kentucky Derby this year, or do you find opposition growing in Louisville?"

Colonel Winn stabbed some of his Waldorf salad with his salad fork. "I'll be honest, Harold. We're in big trouble."

Gladdie leaned forward, glancing from Colonel Winn to Harold Sullivan, balancing a spoonful of soup over her bowl.

"Do you expect an injunction, too, then?" Mr. Breckenridge, the president of the Lexington Jockey Club, asked Colonel Winn.

Winn gulped down the bite of salad from his fork, his brows furrowing. "Unfortunately, I do expect some opposition. We're not sure if we can save the Derby, but I'll not sit by and do nothing."

The Derby...at risk? How could this be? Gladdie exchanged a worried glance with Delia but sipped the soup from her spoon lest she pour it down the front of her gown.

"With the Phoenix cancellation, everyone in Lexington is in a panic. Surely, there must be something that can be done..." Mrs. Breckenridge's voice faded as she reached for a dinner roll.

Gladdie joined others in nodding in emphatic agreement. Even Harvey leaned forward, mouth flattened in apparent concern.

Mary Lou's escort, Thomas, eyed the roll Mrs. Breckenridge buttered. "Would you pass the rolls?"

Mary Lou's brows furrowed as she gazed at her escort. Wasn't Thomas a law clerk? He should know better than to ask for rolls at a time like this, but maybe he didn't understand how serious this was for those in the horseracing industry.

Colonel Winn angled toward Gladdie. "If your

father was here, Gladdie, Joseph would know exactly what to do."

"Yes sir, he would." Gladdie couldn't help but smile weakly in response. It was nice that Colonel Winn remembered her in the middle of all of this. But didn't any of them know what to do?

Delia spoke up with concern in her eyes. "It's probably for the best that Pa isn't here. All of this turmoil would only upset him when he's supposed to be recovering and putting his health first for a change."

"Dinner roll, Gladdie?" Thomas handed her the basket of rolls wrapped in linen.

As she and the colonel on her other side already had bread, Gladdie silently accepted the basket and handed it across the table to Clay, lest he, too, disrupt the conversation over a roll.

"Do you have a plan?" Her grandfather, Colonel Lyndon, asked what everyone else was thinking.

Bravo, Grandfather!

"Would you mind passing the butter?"

Thomas, not again! Gladdie did her best not to release a sigh or roll her eyes. Mary Lou nearly dropped her own butter knife as she stared aghast at her escort. Gladdie spotted a butter dish and passed it to Thomas. Would he keep quiet now? Mary Lou mouthed her a silent *thank you.*

At least Clay appeared to pay close attention. Jake's raised brows showed he also seemed anxious to hear what the president of Churchill Downs had to say. But were any of them as anxious as she was, with her heart beating so fast everyone could surely hear it?

"I believe we do have a plan." Colonel Winn shifted in his seat as he picked up his glass of sweet tea. "We're up against our own new mayor. He's just passed a law prohibiting bookmaking. We think we've found a way around it, but it's kept us up late at night scouring the law books."

Grandfather leaned forward. "What about auction pools?"

In auction pools, bettors bid on their chosen horses, the highest bidder won each horse, and the money would go into a winner-take-all pool for whoever had the winning horse.

Winn shook his head. "We think they'll be outlawed, too, but we did finally find a loophole. Pari-mutuel wagering."

"You mean, machine betting?" Harold Sullivan's brows rose as he stabbed some of his salad.

Colonel Winn nodded, taking a hearty bite of his dinner roll. "Some city officials have tried to block it. But the judge has issued an injunction, allowing it."

"That's wonderful news..." Gladdie dipped her spoon in some of the soup and breathed a sigh of relief. Maybe there was a glimmer of hope, after all.

Colonel Winn nodded, winking at her. "It is, isn't it? The good Lord gave us favor."

Gladdie smiled, sitting up straighter. Couldn't folks see that betting wasn't entirely evil? Even the Israelites drew straws for their inheritance. When people chose to spend more than they should or drink excessively at these events, that was when they became evil. Moderation was key.

She could hardly wait to see Moon Lily race at the Derby. But could it proceed with so many problems before them? Machine betting might not be so easy to implement in such a short time.

As if reading her mind, Colonel Winn finished chewing and waved his roll toward Harold Sullivan. "Only problem is, we've been looking everywhere for Clark's pari-mutuel machines...but no one can seem to find them."

"Oh no, that's terrible. Where could they be?" Mrs. Pickett paused from tasting her soup to stare at Winn.

"That is the question of the century, madam." Colonel Winn punctuated his statement by stabbing an apple in his Waldorf salad.

Grandfather Lyndon suspended his fork with a lettuce leaf perched on the end of it. "You don't mean the ones Merriweather Lewis Clark brought back from Paris, do you?"

Winn wiped a corner of his mouth with his linen napkin. "Yes, I do. He brought back three of them."

"I remember. He once showed me those machines." Grandfather set his fork aside.

"Colonel Lyndon, do you remember where you

were exactly when he showed you?" Winn waited to take another bite of his roll, leaning toward her grandfather with widened eyes. "You may be the only person we know who remembers them."

"Let me think now..." Grandfather's brows scrunched together.

Please help him remember, Lord. When Gladdie opened her eyes, she found that Clay had closed his too. Was he, too, praying for her grandfather? It certainly appeared so. That sweet man. Would she finally see him in her church—tomorrow, perhaps? Had he retained his faith through the years? Yet another question nagging at her soul to save for later.

"He wouldn't have thrown them away, would he?" Harvey pushed his glasses up farther on the bridge of his nose.

Grandfather shook his head. "Oh no. That would have been akin to throwing a dream overboard. I can tell you that for sure. I was only the president of the Lexington Jockey Club for a few years, but during that time, I developed a close friendship with Merriweather Lewis Clark. His uncles, Lewis and Clark, who gave him the tract of land to build the racecourse on, had already blazed a trail to the Pacific by then, but Merriweather and I were going to have lunch one day while the track was being constructed. We drove out to see how construction was coming along. He wanted to ensure that it looked as nice as the one we have here in Lexington. There wasn't any clubhouse yet, you see. And it was in his library at his home before we went to lunch where he showed me the machines. Then we went to the track, and then, lunch."

"I never doubted you would fail to remember where you saw the machines." Grandmother set her soup spoon aside, and a waiter cleared her bowl away. "His memory is razor sharp, even if it was thirty-some years ago."

"But three machines won't be enough." Mrs. Breckenridge slid a pat of butter on a roll. "That is, if you can find them."

Winn cleared his throat. "True, and we'll send someone to have another look at Clark's home. We have an entire search team on it. They could also be hidden away somewhere at Churchill Downs. I have no doubt we'll find them, but Mrs. Breckenridge brings up a good point. We'll need more than three machines, so I have a friend at Coney Island who is going to ship us two more from New York. I also have a team of mechanics on standby to repair Clark's machines if they happen to be in poor condition when we finally locate them."

"A wise idea." Mr. Breckenridge wiped a corner of his mouth.

"May I have another of those rolls and some butter?" Thomas stared at the basket of rolls that had made it around the table twice.

Mary Lou sat up straighter and nearly shot fire out of her eyes at Thomas, but Gladdie reached for the basket and handed it to him with the butter dish.

Mary Lou turned toward Colonel Winn. "Goodness, that's a lot happening behind the scenes, but even five machines hardly seems like enough for the kind of crowd we typically see at the Derby."

Gladdie could not agree more. The lines would be too long. The day would drag on while people stood in line to place their bets. But all Colonel Winn had done thus far inspired her. The man wasn't about to give up, and neither should she where it came to Velvet Brooks.

Colonel Winn sat back in his chair as several waiters began clearing away the first course and preparing to set out the main entrees. "You're absolutely right, Mary Louise. That's why I'm hoping to find someone to set sail for Paris as soon as possible to bring us back several more machines. It's also why we've moved the date of the Derby out this year to give us a few more weeks, but there are some other problems with that plan."

"Such as...?" Gladdie angled toward him.

"Well, there are only one or two manufacturers in the entire world that make these totalizer machines, and they are both on backlog with orders. But if we can find someone we trust to sail to Paris and back in time for the big day, we have a chance of saving the Derby. I've convinced an old friend at the Longchamps track to give me three machines from his racecourse. But he can't give them to us until after the Grand Prix de Paris. It's being moved up this year from July to April because of some construction scheduled in May at Longchamps. They're getting a bigger clubhouse and more rooftop seating. I suppose my friend, Jean-Claude, could ship them, but in view of the situation I'm already facing with the other machines missing…I'd much prefer a special courier to ensure there is no mishandling. What if they are lost or in disrepair by the time they arrive?"

Breckenridge nodded as a waiter placed his next course before him. "A courier is just good sense. You may not be able to find Clark's machines at all."

"Jean-Claude mentioned one other thing in addition to a hefty bank draft to sweeten the deal, since he'll have to order replacements from a backlogged manufacturer." Colonel Winn reached for his tea glass.

"And what would that be?" Breckenridge arched a brow as he surveyed his main entree.

Colonel Winn wore a sly grin and leaned back in his chair. "A bottle of our finest Kentucky bourbon."

Chuckles arose from around the table. Gladdie couldn't help but shake her head and laugh too. If anyone could make the deal work, it was Colonel Winn. Just listening to him talk about all he had to overcome made her head spin.

"Jean-Claude drives a hard bargain," Clay inserted with a sarcastic smile, drawing more smiles and nods in return.

Yet another thing she liked about her escort. He still had that charming way of winning friends that had always drawn her to him.

"You need someone trustworthy to deliver that

bourbon and bring those machines back," Harold Sullivan pointed out.

Mr. Pickett swirled the ice in his glass of tea. "Someone young, adventurous, and energetic enough to want to make an unexpected Atlantic crossing."

More chuckles.

"Someone like Clay here, for instance, who could escort our Gladdie safely across and back again. Chaperoned, of course." Grandmother Lyndon winked at her as the wait staff finished delivering the main course to those at their table.

Gladdie's mouth gaped open. *Oh, Grandmother dear, what* are *you proposing?* But she couldn't get any words of protest to come out. She *had* always envisioned a tour of Europe someday. But, surely, this was only dinner talk and jesting...

"Now, that's a fine idea!" Colonel Winn turned to look at Gladdie as he picked up a dinner fork. "We know Gladdie and Clay can be trusted with those machines." He glanced at Clay, who nodded and grinned, locking eyes on her over the top of flickering candles.

Gladdie's breath caught in her chest. Maybe they weren't jesting, after all. Colonel Winn placed a heavy burden of faith and trust upon their shoulders. Clay certainly seemed as if he wanted to do this...

But how could she join him on an Atlantic crossing? She'd have to sell a horse or something of great value to even afford her fare...not to mention the need for resolution in their fragile relationship. Would she and Clay even be more than friends after the ball? Could they possibly be of help in saving the Derby of 1908? And if so, how could she let all of Kentucky down?

Her head was spinning. It was all happening so fast.

"How is the construction coming on your beautiful home, Clay? I counted at least eight pillars across the front...if my eyes did not deceive me." Mr. Breckenridge smirked at Gladdie's escort.

And now everyone at the table would assume Clay could afford to set sail for Europe. After all, most of them had passed Clay's mansion on the way to Sullivan Hill, and by now, some of them had likely heard rumors of his elevated financial status.

"It's coming along fine. Thank you for asking." Clay sliced into his ham with mint sauce.

Colonel Winn tried some of his roasted duck. "This is much bigger than simply saving the Derby." He went on with enthusiasm as if Mr. Breckenridge had never inserted his question. "Clay and Gladdie represent the next generation, the future of the horseracing industry —a legacy in and of itself. And if these young folk are serious about helping us save the Kentucky Derby, and serious about giving others hope that the industry can not only grow, but thrive, then they have only to let me know within a few days." He glanced up at Clay and then turned toward Gladdie. "Just don't wait too long. The window is closing to get those machines here in time."

The smile on Clay's face told her everything she needed to know. Apparently, he didn't mind rearranging his schedule for a quick jaunt to Europe and back.

Staring at her, Clay sat up straighter. "We'll certainly give it some serious consideration, sir. It's been a few years since I've been to Europe, so I wouldn't mind traveling there again."

He'd been to Europe? Of course he had. He was a gentleman of means now. She still had much to learn about this man who'd been the son of a deceased coal miner when she'd first met him.

"Good, good. Glad to hear it." Colonel Winn reached for the crystal shaker of salt. "Churchill Downs would compensate you for the inconvenience, of course, but those are terms we could discuss later. What do you say we enjoy the rest of the evening, now that we have a potential plan to keep Kentucky on the map in the horseracing world?"

Mrs. Breckenridge pushed her salad plate aside. "But one more thing, Colonel Winn, if I may be so bold as to remind everyone here that this is history in the making. You should consider sending Harvey along to document the journey from start to finish..."

Harvey cocked his head to one side.

Harvey, accompany them? Gladdie quickly smoothed out the frown that attempted to steal over her face. Perhaps now that Clay had escorted her tonight, Harvey had given up his hopes of her.

Colonel Winn thumped the table. "You're absolutely right. What a sensation that would make. Worldwide headlines—I can see now. It could be the catalyst we need to make Churchill Downs and the Derby stand out as one of the best in horseracing once and for all."

Harvey pushed his glasses up on his nose. "The *Lexington Gazette* would probably jump for a chance at an exclusive series of articles about all of this."

When everyone at the table raised their iced tea and punch glasses in agreement to the proposed plan, bringing an end to an intriguing discussion, Gladdie had no choice but to raise her glass too. Her eyes wide, she stared at the roast beef on her plate. *What are You up to now, Lord?*

Breathless from dancing in Clay's arms through two more waltzes after dinner, Gladdie exhaled a sigh of relief when he returned with her to their seats. He offered to fetch glasses of punch and disappeared into the crowd toward the refreshment table. While an intermission began to give musicians and dancers alike a rest, she snapped open and employed her fan, determined to ignore the whispers and stares brought on by her dancing so much with her escort. No one said anything, though, probably assuming Clay intended to propose soon.

Her stomach tightened at the notion. Would his explanation of the past enable her to accept?

For the moment, Harvey and Colonel Winn seemed engrossed in a discussion she'd give anything to hear. Grandfather Lyndon glanced toward them and rose from his seat beside her grandmother, who was presently engaged in a conversation with Mrs. Pickett. Was he going to join the men? But no, he turned toward her and sat down in Clay's empty seat.

She smiled at him while fluttering her fan. "Hello, Grandfather. Enjoying the ball?"

He nodded, stretching out one leg. "I am. And you?"

She returned an affectionate smile. "A wonderful evening..."

Grandfather crossed his arms over his chest and leaned back in his seat. "I'll admit, I had my doubts after hearing about that race in town against Thaddeus, but Clay Grinstead seems to have turned into a fine gentleman."

She followed his gaze toward the refreshment table where her escort waited in a line of other gentlemen eager to ladle out cups of punch for their dance partners. "I'm still determining whether or not that is a true assessment, but it does seem to be the case."

"Good. I believe it may very well be a case worthy of your consideration." He patted her hand. "I hope you have a fine rest of the evening. Your grandmother and I will be departing soon...but we'll see you tomorrow at church."

She angled to grasp the expression in his eyes as he rose to return to his seat. Did her grandfather mean to impart some tidbit of wisdom concerning her escort's character? He'd been the one to rescue her all those years ago on that fateful night, so his opinion meant more than anyone's. And clearly, he now offered his stamp of approval. She couldn't help but smile as their eyes met briefly. "Thank you, Grandfather. See you tomorrow."

Aurelia and Callie sat together a few seats over to her right, perhaps waiting for their dance partners to return with more punch too. Farther down, Delia and Jake spoke to another couple. Then Mary Lou suddenly filled Gladdie's vision, sinking into Clay's empty seat—with tears brimming in her eyes!

"What's wrong, Mary Lou? Where's Thomas?" Gladdie's gaze swept the sea of guests, finding him speaking with some other debutante, and a much younger one, wearing a very beautiful gown.

"I wish he was more like your Clay, so chivalrous and attentive." She sniffed, swiping tears away. "He has only danced with me once this whole evening, even though he knows I've been saving dances for him."

What could she do to comfort her friend? She reached for her purse and unsnapped the clasp, withdrawing her handkerchief. "Here, take this and dry your eyes."

Mary Lou did as she instructed. A few moments later, she caught Thomas glancing at Mary Lou, tilting his head with a thoughtful gleam in his eye. "Ah, I think he's coming your way now. Try and smile. Look happy."

Mary Lou nodded and straightened, curving her lips upward a little.

Unfortunately, Clay's attention and behavior toward Gladdie had been so lavish that it had drawn the admiration of her friend, and likely others in the younger set too. To the point that Mary Lou would risk admonishment for dancing too much with the same dance partner, thereby defying conventional standards. That would only upset Mrs. Sullivan. Gladdie at least had a history with Clay and an unspoken understanding, whereas her dear friend risked much more with her new beau, an outsider to the horseracing community. It might be for the best if Thomas did not ask her to dance quite so much as Clay had Gladdie, but one or two more dances would go a long way toward helping her friend enjoy the evening.

Thomas approached and stood before Mary Lou. He bowed toward Gladdie and then returned his gaze to her friend. "May I have the next dance after the intermission, Mary Lou?"

Gladdie smiled, and Mary Lou perked up. "Oh, Thomas! I thought you'd never ask…"

Clay returned with their punch and handed Gladdie a glass, taking in the scene as she sipped some of the liquid. "Did I miss anything?"

Laughter rose from Callie and Aurelia, giggling behind a paper that they hid behind, their heads bent close together. Gladdie raised an eyebrow before turning back to Clay. "No. I think I'm ready to step outside for some fresh air before the next dance. Shall we take a turn on the balcony?"

"Your wish is my command." Clay extended his hand, pulling her up and onto her feet.

"I'll see you later, Mary Louise." She waved to her friend, who waved back, a smile on her face now that Thomas, who hovered nearby, had risen to her expectations.

Clay held onto Gladdie's hand, leading the way toward the balcony doors. He navigated them through the other guests, and soon they stepped outside where the balcony overlooked an immense span of gardens behind the main house. When they reached the stone balustrade railing, they leaned against it, gazing up at the starry night sky.

"It's such a beautiful night. All of the stars are visible." She kept her voice to a whisper, drinking in their peaceful surroundings as he placed a hand over hers.

"I think they are winking at us, smiling down on us with their sparkling shimmers." Clay's face grew serious as he gazed up at the stars, standing so close she could smell his cologne. "How amazing that the Lord hung them, suspended them in the heavens, commanded them to stay, and that they obey Him after thousands of years."

She smiled, recognizing the reference to a Psalm. "And that even the waters of the sea obey the boundaries He gave them." Clearly, he was still nourishing his faith, reading the Word, contemplating the deep and wonderful things of God.

He turned toward her, pulling her close, then planting a tender kiss on her lips. "Are you having a good evening?"

Nodding, she smiled, her gloved hand resting over his heart, detecting the rapid beat. She was, and she couldn't find words in the English language to convey the glimmer of hope rising in her heart, the inspiration Colonel Winn had given her, or the outstanding impression Clay had made on her throughout the evening by his attentiveness and excellent manners. Did holding her in his arms give him as much of a thrill as it gave her to be held by him?

The intermission came to an end as musicians returned to the stage, where they tuned their instruments. Then another waltz poured through the open French doors.

Clay smiled wistfully. "Ah, this is a favorite melody of mine. Do you know it?"

She tilted her ear toward the ballroom, and her face lit up. "It's called *Girl of My Dreams*."

"Shall we dance out here, just the two of us?" Clay's brow lifted, and he held up his arms, inviting her to dance with him on the balcony under the stars, bathed in a golden swath of moonlight. She nodded, placing her hand in his and the other on his arm. He led her in time to the melody, swirling her around at all of the right times, holding her close other times, his hand strong and comforting on her back.

When the dance ended, he rested his chin in her hair. "How I've missed you..."

"And I you," she whispered.

But what would he tell her when their fairytale night came to an end?

CHAPTER FOURTEEN

Casting all your care upon Him; for He careth for you.
—I Peter 5:7, KJV

Carter drove them home after the last dance. When Gladdie settled into the open carriage beside Clay, she angled toward him. "I have a request."

"Name it, and unto the half of the kingdom, I will give it thee." He grinned.

"I'd like to speak with you in the library before you go home."

His brow arched and then he laughed. "I was going to ask the same question."

Within half an hour, she sat in her favorite chair in Pa's library and Clay on the sofa directly across from her, each of them clutching a mug of hot chocolate

Gladdie had managed to make them while rummaging about in the dimly lit kitchen. Meanwhile, he had built a fire in the fireplace. It crackled as the flames flickered, casting a warm glow on everything. Finally, they could chat without interruption.

He rose and brought her shawl, and now he draped it around her shoulders. "I can't have you catching a chill."

She didn't protest, but she did kick off her heeled shoes as he returned to his seat on the sofa. Her feet ached from dancing all night. They sipped the soothing refreshment for a few moments, but a glance at her purse laying on the table with the oil lamp and tray beside her chair reminded her of the importance of her question. Her hands shook so much that she had to set the cocoa aside. Best dive into it.

"Tell me, Clay, tell me what happened that night when you didn't come to marry me as we had planned and as you had promised. When I waited for you at the Lexington train station, and then later in the pouring rain on the porch of the house where the justice of the peace lived in Richmond. I went ahead and took the train, assuming you'd eventually make it there. Why didn't you? I'll never understand why you simply abandoned me, far from home, with no idea what had happened." There, she'd asked it, the question to which she dreaded hearing the answer. Now he would tell her that he'd fallen in love with Alice...

Clay grimaced. "That was wretched of me, I know.

But I wasn't sure if you'd decided to take the train when I wasn't able to make it to the depot. I had no way of knowing for sure. And with that thunderstorm, I wasn't even sure you'd make it to Lexington. My family lived so much closer to the station." He heaved a sigh, his chest expanding and then sinking as his shoulders sagged.

She crossed her arms and sank deeper into Pa's chair. "I rode Marigold all the way to the station in that deluge."

He raked a hand through his hair, some strands loosening from the evening's careful pomade. "I was ready to head to the train station, too, when the telephone rang. I had packed a small satchel with the barest of necessities, and I waited while my stepfather answered, thinking, what if it was you on the other end of the line? What if something had caused you a delay? What if you were calling me from Sullivan Hill or some other telephone? But it wasn't you. It was Senator Parker, Alice's father. Then Otto came upstairs to my room, banging on my door, shouting that we had to go fetch Cora."

"Cora?" She raised her brows and tilted her head.

Before his disappearance with Alice, Clay had talked to Gladdie a few times about the problems concerning Cora. Losing their brother Cadence to a high fever and then losing their pa, Abraham, about a year later from some type of lung disease after a lifetime of working in the coal mines—on top of the financial chaos that had ensued and added responsibilities of helping their mother—had taken a toll on the remaining siblings, especially Clay's impressionable younger sister, the elder of his two sisters.

At seventeen, Cora had been spurned by one of her suitors. She had lost touch with reality and streaked down Main Street in her unmentionables. She'd broken dishes, refused to comply with reasonable requests, and exhibited belligerence to anyone in authority in her life. Finally, her stepfather had put his foot down and sent her to the asylum to spare Clay's mother, Eula, and the whole family any other gut-wrenching incidents and the gossip that always followed.

He drew in a deep breath. "Yes, Cora. She had escaped from the Lexington asylum that night—wearing her underthings again, mind you. Somehow, she ended up on the Parkers' front lawn, dancing in the rain. Judge Parker, Alice's grandfather, saw her from inside the Parker mansion. A judge! He could have had her placed in custody or taken to jail for disturbing the peace."

"Go on." Her eyes wide, she encouraged him softly, hands wrapped around her mug. The Parkers had always lived in a nicer area than Clay's nearby older neighborhood. The senator and his father had shared their three-story home with its beautiful limestone walls and enormous front porch, whereas Clay lived in a more modest, dark-red brick two-story. Close enough to walk past Alice's house every day on the way home from school. Something Gladdie had considered for years.

"Otto insisted I help him retrieve Cora from the Parker family's front lawn." Clay's somber expression as he gazed toward the floor while he spoke tugged on Gladdie's heart. "And he said Senator Ezra Parker had said something about speaking to us privately. I had no idea about what. Neither did Otto. I just knew I wasn't going to make the train and there wasn't anything I could do about it. My mother was crying and carrying on about how we'd be ruined, and my stepfather was hollering and making demands. I kept saying I had to be somewhere, but they would hear none of it. Otto grabbed my collar and shoved me up against the wall. He said I would come now and help him or else my mother would end up just like Cora from the shame."

She scooted closer to the edge of her seat. "It sounds wretched."

"It was." He paused, drawing in another breath. "We hitched up the buggy, and Otto and I headed to the Parker home. And there were Cora, the senator, and the judge in the front yard, playing a game of cat and mouse. Each time one of them managed to get close to her, she ran in another direction, laughing her head off. At least they had managed to keep her there until we arrived."

Gladdie ran her hand over her face, cringing as she imagined Clay's embarrassment.

"The four of us managed to wrangle her inside the

house. She clawed and scratched all of us pretty good. Mrs. Parker—Elsie, the senator's wife—helped us calm her down and made her tea. And there she sat in one of the finest homes in Lexington, in the parlor, in her soaking wet undergarments, having tea with a senator's wife and a judge's wife, as if nothing had happened." He cringed. "Mrs. Parker covered her with a blanket, and the judge and senator told Otto and me to come with them to the judge's study."

Gladdie angled toward Clay and tucked her feet under her ball gown, digesting the story he'd shared so far. No wonder Clay hadn't shown up. But why hadn't he come later, after they settled Cora down and returned her to the asylum?

Clay shifted on the sofa, the muscles in his jaw clenching. "So then we sat down in Woodrow's study... the judge, Alice's grandfather. He said they had a problem, and we had a problem, but that we could help each other."

"What was their problem, and what did Judge Parker suggest?" Gladdie's brows rose.

"He informed us that Alice was pregnant out of wedlock from some other suitor who wasn't going to do the right thing by marrying her."

She released a small gasp, covering her mouth. So he hadn't been in love with Alice, after all—at least not when they married.

He continued, his shoulders visibly taut through his white shirt and vest now that he had shed his cutaway jacket. "They were facing the ruin of their good standing in society, and they believed Alice had no future left if they didn't marry her off to someone quickly. Judge Parker said he understood we had been shamed time and again by society because of Cora, and that we were dealing with her being locked up somewhere she didn't want to be. They guessed rightly that it was breaking my mother's heart and traumatizing the whole family."

"I remember you mentioning your mother's sorrow over all of this." She sipped some of her hot chocolate.

With downcast eyes, he kept his voice low. "Judge Parker said they could offer me what they had offered to the other suitor—an estate they rarely used, Amber Hall, on the outskirts of Richmond. A modest spread with a main house and a guest house where my family could live. They suggested that Otto could retire from keeping books for the railroad and move my mother and sisters there. They could sell the house here in Lexington that my biological father had worked for and tuck the proceeds in the bank as additional retirement funds."

"I can see where that would provide much-needed security." Had she offered enough compassion in her tone? Even from what he'd shared so far, she could now imagine the ordeal he'd suffered.

"Right. My parents and Callie could live in the main house, and Cora could live in the guest house with round-the-clock staff to provide quality personal and medical care. My mother could visit her every day. Callie and Otto could visit too. The judge suggested they keep a low profile in hopes of leading a happy life, free from rumors so Callie wouldn't become a social outcast. And as you may remember, things had been heading in that direction for my family." He paused and drank some of his hot chocolate.

"I do." She recalled all too well the number of times Cora and Callie had been left out of various social circles and activities at their finishing school. She'd always done her best to include them, but rumors had hampered their popularity and acceptance before Cora went to the asylum. After, it hadn't been much better for Callie. And she'd faced the hardships alone.

Gladdie looked down at her mug, finally beginning to see the whole picture. "But they wanted you to marry Alice...in exchange for Cora's medical care and Amber Hall."

The grim expression on his face and the truth of his story began to break down the remaining walls in her heart. "Yes. That's how Amber Hall would remain in the family. It was an estate handed down through the generations to Elsie, Senator Parker's wife, my former mother-in-law. But Senator Parker assured us his wife cared more about Alice's future and their reputation than having the use of that estate. They were all planning to retire in New York anyhow."

"I see. So that's where they all moved to...and you, with Alice." She tilted her head as he nodded. "Seems as though they came up with a plan in only a few minutes after discovering Cora in their yard. That part doesn't quite make sense to me. They had already planned to speak to you about this before you even arrived...I mean, how do you explain that?"

"Yes, they had figured all of this out somewhere between the time she turned up in their yard and when they telephoned us. They were quite open about the fact that they had recently made the same offer to Alice's beau, Emmett Tristan, but he'd turned it all down. He would already inherit a big house in Lexington, and his family owned a successful law practice. He was determined to marry some other lady. And he had no issues to hide as my family had. Of course, Otto was adamant I take the offer if I cared anything at all for my family."

"And so Emmett Tristan is Olympia's father?" She'd met some of the Tristan family at an annual horse auction some years ago, but because the encounter had been brief, she'd had no opinion of them...until now. What kind of man would take advantage of a woman and turn his back on her and their child?

With a nod, he set his mug aside and buried his hands in his face. When he looked up, he flattened his mouth. "You're the only person left alive on the earth who knows that other than her father, Emmett himself, who has never bothered to look into her existence. And Otto, or course. Olympia doesn't even know, and with help from God, I hope and pray she never has to know."

It was clear how much he cared for Ollie, the little one he sometimes called Olive. "It would be devastating for her to discover all of that. Your secret is safe with me."

"Yes, it would be devastating. You deserve to know, which is why I am telling you." He reached across from the sofa and patted her hand. "And I trust you."

A twinge of remorse surged through her heart. Because she hadn't been able to return that trust. She could do much better now, knowing more of the story. "So all of this time, you have been paying for round-the-clock medical care for Cora? Has she improved?"

He cocked his head to one side. "Yes, I've been paying for her medical care, but she isn't much better from what I understand, though I'm told she is happier there than in an asylum. And my mother and Otto are much happier about the situation. I'm told she has good and bad days, but I haven't seen the rest of my family in years...since that fateful night the Parkers and Otto cornered me into marrying Alice. Alice didn't want to get involved with Cora, so we were never able to visit."

Gladdie's mouth dropped open. "You haven't seen your mother or stepfather all of these years? She must have a broken heart of another sort, missing her first-born son."

"Sadly, no, I haven't seen her. It's part of why I allowed Callie to join me here, because I do miss them, but we have exchanged letters and made a few telephone calls. As for paying for the medical care, they offered me a vice president's position at Parker Mines in New York—and an impressive salary to go with it. Of course, they promised there would be plenty left over to provide for Alice and her child, and any other children we might have with the kind of life Alice would be accustomed to—as in, the best of everything. And they kept that promise. My salary has always covered all of Cora's medical care and everything else."

"So, all of these years, you've sacrificed your whole future and all of your hopes and dreams to pay for medical care for Cora...and to keep her out of an asylum? And you've been letting your family live at Amber Hall without charging them anything for it. And you haven't even been able to visit your own mother and sisters, or your stepfather." Her heart squeezed from merely considering the blow he'd been dealt.

"That about sums it up. The judge, Alice's grandfather, married us in his study that evening." He released a sigh and sank back into the sofa.

Now it all made so much more sense. How final that sounded. And how awful he must have felt all of these years. As terrible as it had been for her, his lot had been even harsher. She couldn't possibly give Clay that letter now. None of this had been his fault.

"They sent us by train to New York the very next morning, to live near Parker Mines. The rest of the Parkers joined us there several months later. We all lived on a grand estate, and I did my best under the circumstances. But on the inside, I was devastated, losing you, the one person I loved—and losing my family in many ways. There wasn't a day that went by that I didn't think of you. I wrote to you. Didn't you receive my letter?" One of his brows arched.

"No, I never received a letter." She frowned. What had become of it? Had it arrived and perhaps her mother had tossed it, hoping to keep her mind off the situation?

He tugged on his cravat, loosening it, briefly waving his other hand, palm up. "That explains why you've been upset for so long, thinking I was too callous to even bother to send an explanation. I don't know what happened to the letter, but I did send one."

She bit her lower lip. "If I had received it, I'm sure it would have helped me to understand."

Clay shifted to sit on the edge of the sofa and reached across to her as she perched on Pa's favorite chair, taking her hand in his again. "If we had married, everything would have been different. We would have visited both of our families. We'd have worked hard to build our own life. But Cora...she'd probably still be in that asylum. In the end, the one thing I kept hearing in my head that night were the words my father had spoken to me on his deathbed, when he'd asked me to look after my mother and sisters. I was only twelve when he died, and the weight of that promise is a heavy burden I carry to this day. What I did was the only way to spare Cora from a life of misery. And it was the only way to spare my mother and sister from being parted from her."

She'd driven past the Lexington asylum in Pa's carriage many a time, always in a quandary over what had become of Cora and Clay and his family. The place looked like a prison or a hospital, only with a garden. And a tad more eerie. A miserable place for anyone, really. No one liked hospitals…or prisons.

Having the burden of Velvet Brooks on her shoulders the past few months, she could understand the sense of responsibility he carried. All she could do was let him continue to hold her hand, a sweet gesture that not so very long ago would have repulsed her. Now, her heart swelled with compassion for all that he'd sacrificed and the honorable decision he'd made. She supposed she would have done the same in his shoes.

He squeezed her hand. "But I lost you in the process, a huge price to pay. And for a while, I lost my faith, too, at an even greater price, which has only begun to restore since having you in my life again. I felt God had asked too much of me all those years. Though I guess I would do it all over again if it was going to keep Cora out of the asylum. Not just for Cora's sake, but my mother's sake, and Callie's sake…"

Gladdie tilted her head. Yes. In a way, her suffering had also been for the good of his family. Only, she'd had to suffer as a blind, trusting servant to the Lord, not knowing why. Hadn't the Messiah also been an unquestioning servant, coming to the earth and to die on the cross for the sins of the world?

She wiped a tear away. "No, I don't suppose anyone could have turned that kind of help away in the face of all those medical and emotional needs." Sitting up straighter, she withdrew her hand from him. "But I dearly hope your renewed faith does not rest solely upon my return to you, though I am greatly encouraged by all you have shared, and for the first time, I can say there may be hope for us, after all." So long as prayer confirmed it, she could now permit him to pursue her romantically.

His blue eyes brightened. "No, I won't make the mistake of giving up my faith again. I admit, it feels good to cast my cares on the Lord after all of these years of doing things my way and relying upon myself instead of Him."

She smiled at this confession. "It's true that the Lord always knows best when He asks us for obedience, action, commitment, or a sacrifice of some sort." Did He not always have her best interests and the interests of others at heart? Had He not brought her through her heartbreak, giving her the dream of owning a school for orphans someday, and a loving, close-knit family to love her through her affliction?

But there was another question she dreaded to ask, but must. "And so all the Parkers have died, and you've inherited everything, and you have your freedom at long last. But...Alice...how did she die? And when?"

"She died a year ago, giving birth to what would have been Ollie and Emery's little brother...a shock to all of us, losing them both at once." He stared at the crackling flames in the fireplace. "One thing I've learned, life can be hard, messy, and plain old awful at times. But we have to be strong and make the best of it, or life will knock you down if you let it."

"That's dreadful, losing them both at once. I'm sorry to hear this too." She could hardly imagine it, him having to lay them to rest at one time. No doubt, he'd done his best to offer stability to Alice and give her a good life. But now, his children lacked a mother and a sibling they would never get to know on this side of heaven.

Turning his gaze on her, he offered a weak smile. "Yes, but if that hadn't happened, I wouldn't have had the chance to regain the only woman I ever truly loved. And as you said, I am now finally free. Free to forge a new life of my own choosing." He drew her hand to his lips and kissed it gently with a brush of his lips.

Could he see her blush in the flickering light that enveloped them? "And your inheritance must be some comfort in the face of all of this loss. But 'to whom much is given, much is required.'"

"There is that. God works in mysterious ways. I plan to use it wisely. And now, I can share that inheritance with you. Anything at all that you need or desire... please, just let me know. I can help you insulate Velvet Brooks from the turmoil in the racing world. Together, we can help save the Derby if you want, too, as Colonel Winn suggested. We can go to Paris and get those machines. Why not? I'm free at last, and with you by my side, and the Lord on our side, we can do anything." Rising, he pulled her to her feet. "But I must go. It's late. You need your rest, and it'd be nice to be in church tomorrow without falling asleep during the sermon. But I do pray this has given you a fresh perspective of the past and the pain I've caused you."

She hid her eyes from him, but raising her chin, she tilted her head to one side. "It has softened the blow a great deal. I need to let it all sink in. We have much to consider concerning everything Colonel Winn mentioned too..."

He nodded. "And our future."

"Yes, our future." Her voice was a whisper, but she offered him a warm smile so he would rest well and have hope in her after how much she had pushed him away in recent weeks. She could finally release the tension about Clay Grinstead, but it would take some time to digest all he'd shared.

"I don't want to remember any of it, but as I said, you deserved to know. And on that note, I hope you had a wonderful evening, all things considered."

"I did. Thank you. It was lovely. A nearly perfect evening."

He smiled, brushing a lock of hair from her eyes. "May I sit beside you in church tomorrow and afterwards, give you a tour of Hickory Chase?"

"Hickory Chase? Is that the name you've chosen for your newest estate?" A good name for a horse farm, causing her face to light up. Looking toward their future seemed much happier than discussing the sordid past. "And yes, you may sit beside me in church."

"Yes, it is. Do you like it?" His brow arched.

"Like it? I love it!"

"Good. I thought you might. May I kiss you good night? And then I'll show myself out."

Heat warmed her cheeks, but she smiled. "Yes, you may kiss me."

He pulled her into his arms for a long, intense kiss. And when he let her go, was the room spinning?

Lifting her hand to his lips, he kissed it once more, earning another smile from her. "Good night, my darling Gladiola."

"Good night, Clay." She couldn't tear her gaze away from him as he stepped out into the hall. The front door opened and closed softly. And she sank with wobbly knees into the chair, holding a hand to her lips where he'd kissed her only moments ago, leaving her dizzy and reeling, her heart pounding with excitement.

The man had shouldered so much. She couldn't possibly walk away from him.

But could he restore and improve relationships where his family was concerned? Though Callie seemed to cheer Clay up, she wanted for some guidance as she matured, needing a companion and lacking the wherewithal to look after his children so that he'd had to reinstate a nanny, and he still needed to reconnect with his parents and Cora. Only in time could Gladdie be assured of Clay's ability to navigate his family relationships. But perhaps she could help him.

She reached for her purse and opened it. Time to destroy that letter in the fireplace and embrace her future with Clay.

But where was it?

She rummaged through the small handbag, but there was no sign of it. She turned the evening purse upside down and let the few contents tumble out onto her lap.

No folded paper. Was it inside the invitation? She turned it upside down and shook it too. No, not there.

She had been so careful to not extract it when reading Clay the menu. Had she dropped it somewhere, perhaps when she had offered Mary Lou the handkerchief? Was it somewhere on the floor of the Sullivan ballroom? And if not, who might have it? It simply could not fall into Clay's possession after all that man had suffered.

Her mouth dropped open as she recalled Aurelia and Callie laughing as they'd hidden behind something they'd been reading...

No, no, no...this most dreadful turn of events could not possibly be happening!

CHAPTER FIFTEEN

When my soul fainted within me, I remembered the Lord: And my prayer came in unto thee, into thine holy temple.
—Jonah 2:7, KJV

MARCH 18, 1908

FIRST CHRISTIAN CHURCH, LEXINGTON, KENTUCKY

Sleep had evaded Gladdie until she sought peace from the Lord concerning the missing letter, but the next morning on the way to church, and even after she had settled in beside Clay on the pew, she had to remind herself that with His help, she would somehow weather this storm. The Holy Spirit knew all things. He could lead her to recover what she had penned before

Clay laid eyes on it...or help her find a way to survive the ordeal with her new relationship intact.

The sermon about four unclean beggars who took a chance in visiting the camp of the enemy army rather than entering the famine-struck city of Jerusalem during a siege caused Gladdie's heart to soar. When the lepers arrived at the Syrian camp, they found Israel's enemies had abandoned their tents, leaving a goldmine of riches to be plundered. This was her encouragement, the answer to her prayers about taking a second chance on Clay, something else she had diligently sought the Lord about.

While others yawned who'd attended the ball the night before, she could hardly peel her eyes from the preacher, hanging on every word. Clay's reassuring arm around her shoulder may have caused a few tongues to wag, but she didn't care. And how sweet it had been to sing worship songs with his children taking turns to steal little glances at her, sometimes even looking up at her adoringly.

After the service, Clay introduced her to Nanny Tuddlesworth, a lady who lived up to her name with her efficient demeanor and plump figure. While the nanny and children piled into his Roadster, he escorted Gladdie to her buggy, helped her climb inside, and handed the reins over.

He leaned on the side of the conveyance with a sheepish look on his face. "Uh, um, I'm not sure what you'll think of this. It's rather spontaneous..." He scratched behind one ear. "Delia's cook offered to prepare a picnic lunch for us for this afternoon. I thought we could eat it at Hickory Chase—that is, if you approve. She promised roast beef sandwiches, cold fried potatoes, and apple rhubarb pie."

"That sounds delicious. I am anxious for that tour you promised." She smiled at him, holding the reins steady with one gloved hand, smoothing her peach frock with the other. She was weary of eating so many meals alone at Velvet Brooks with her folks away. An impromptu picnic sounded nice. After all, she'd given Willamena the day off, intending to heat some leftovers.

He hesitated, one brow arching. "Only one problem. Aurelia and Callie said they are dying to see the inside of the house too. I'll tell them to come along some other time if you prefer."

Her eyes widened as she stared at her horse, currently flicking his tail, ready to be on the way. Would the girls have the note in their possession? Perhaps she could simply ask for it back. She turned to look at him slowly. "You don't say? How nice. Do tell them to join us, but I'll have to meet you there in an hour. I'll need time to change and freshen up. Will Olive and Emery be there?"

"Fine. No, umm, the children are having lunch with their nanny and then taking their Sunday afternoon naps, but I'll meet you there. I think the perfect place for our picnic will be inside on the second floor in the sitting room. It has the nicest view of the front lawn. There aren't any furnishings yet, but I'll bring a quilt."

"That sounds nice." It would be a full afternoon—seeing his home, enjoying a picnic lunch with him, and even more important right now...the chance to retrieve the note she never should have written in the first place.

"Perhaps we can take a private stroll on the grounds afterwards, and I can show you more of the property." He smiled, leaning closer. "I'd kiss you, but then we'd scandalize the church folk."

"I don't think I'd mind." She smiled at him, gazing into those sky-blue eyes. "Clay...?"

"Yes?" His brows rose.

"I think if we go to Europe, we should take sweet Olive and Emery so I can get to know them a little better." She bit her lower lip. Would he set her mind at ease by prioritizing family relationships even before she made the ultimate commitment to him?

His brows furrowed. "I don't. You and I have some lost time to make up for. They'll be fine with the nanny for a few weeks."

"Well, I disagree. And another thing...we should go and see your parents." She pulled her gloves on more snugly.

Crease lines appeared on his forehead. "I'm not sure if we have the time to go to Richmond right now *and* save the Derby. Besides, I'm not certain I'm ready for that."

"Clay, I'm sure your absence is absolutely breaking

your mother's heart..." She turned her most imploring gaze upon him.

He sighed. "I'll think about it. I do intend to see them, and soon, but there is just so much happening so fast right now."

"Which is why we should continue to take things slowly and methodically." Didn't he understand how important it was to mend his relationship with his mother? Gladdie couldn't even imagine a wedding without his parents there, though he had yet to officially propose...but he had talked about his intention of marrying her.

"You set the pace. I'm fine with slow and methodical," he assured her. "Today is just a picnic and a tour of the house, but I'll give this some thought."

"Very good." Good enough for now. She blew him a kiss from her gloved palm.

He grinned at her, tipping his hat. "See you in a little while."

She nodded. "See you soon."

He straightened and patted the side of the buggy, stepping back to give her room to pull away. Perhaps he would kiss her on their stroll...

She snapped the reins, and the smart-looking dapple gray carried her toward home. But as the horse trotted along, suspicions nagged at her, and a knot grew in her stomach. Callie and Aurelia hadn't attended morning worship. Judging by their laughter at the ball, they were up to no good, plotting against her somehow.

And if that was the case, they weren't going to simply hand over that note.

No, they might well be concocting a plan to inform Clay that Gladdie could not be trusted, giving Aurelia a chance with him. Callie could assume the role of a hero to her brother, and Aurelia would convince him she was far more loyal than Gladdie.

She couldn't let that happen. But she required a convincing reason they should give her the letter. And she had an outrageous idea.

Forty minutes later, Gladdie surveyed her appearance in the oval mirror in her bedroom. Would her disguise work? She'd tied one of Mama's pillows over the front of her corset with some twine from the old tool shed. She'd tied another pillow from the linen closet to her bottom. It had taken quite a bit of twine to accomplish those tasks.

She'd then borrowed a pillow from the guest room and cut it in half. Despite a mess of down feathers covering her quilt, she'd stuffed most of the feathers from each half into two flour sacks from the kitchen and tied the ends. Then she'd tied the flour sacks stuffed with feathers to her arms. No easy task, but she could now pass for a lady with a rather plump silhouette. Although, she needed larger outer garments and another layer of petticoats. Nothing in her wardrobe would fit over her new figure. Not even Mama was this robust.

However, Grace had been gathering extra maternity clothing for Delia's pregnancy. Most of the items were those Veronica and a few other ladies in the community had discarded. Grace would hardly miss anything if Gladdie borrowed a few things from the neatly folded pile awaiting more donations on the kitchen worktable.

She wrapped a sheet from the linen closet around herself lest anyone enter the house and find her in such a state, and breezed downstairs to the kitchen, her heels clicking as she clutched the sheet to her neckline.

Gladdie rummaged through the pile on the worktable, selecting a petticoat with a generous waist and a roomy, high-collared white shirtwaist. Torn between a black skirt and a walking suit, she settled on the plaid, two-piece ensemble consisting of a coat that flared at the waist and a rather large skirt in a shade of pastel mint green with a great many gathers. The mint green and soft pink shades might work well with her mother's most ostentatious hat. Smiling at her ingenuity, she hurried back upstairs with the items, conscious of her window of time running out. Goodness, she really must hurry.

After donning the clothing, to make her face look older, she mixed some face powder with a tube of neutral paint from Veronica's former bedroom until she had a paste concoction resembling skin color. Her sister wouldn't mind if she borrowed one of her old palettes for a crisis of this nature.

She slathered it on with one of Veronica's paint brushes, heavily enough to create a layer of older-looking skin, then snapped her fan open to dry the concoction. Messy, but effective. She barely recognized herself.

Brushing on some more white powder helped seal the layer in place and gave her an elderly lady complexion and a fuller face. She used her finger to add a few wrinkle lines and surveyed the result. Matronly enough...

She twisted her hair into a tight bun at the nape of her neck and flew to the attic, raiding Mama's costume trunk where she kept all sorts of items for masquerade balls and a few skits they had performed over the years. Finding the white wig she and her sisters had used to portray George Washington, Martha Washington, and Marie Antoinette on various occasions, she donned the curly mass, tugging until it was in place.

She ran to Mama's mirror. Perfect! After pinning a wide-brimmed hat with a plethora of pink flowers in place—too many, perhaps—and swiping and sliding on Pa's wire-rimmed reading glasses, she stood back to assess her completed look.

Hello, Aunt Bertha!

Not too terrible of a plan, considering how little time she'd had to come up with something. One day, maybe she'd write in her journal about how she'd invented Aunt Bertha in under an hour. Speaking of which...

She glanced at her timepiece. Barely four minutes left to make it to Hickory Chase. She'd take the buggy waiting by the veranda.

Now to convince Aurelia and Callie that Gladdie's estranged, wealthy Aunt Bertha had arrived to stop her niece from marrying Clay and that she needed their help. Then perhaps they would hand over that note.

CHAPTER SIXTEEN

Fear thou not; for I am with thee: be not dismayed; for I
am thy God: I will strengthen thee; yea, I will help thee;
yea, I will uphold thee with the right
hand of my righteousness.
—Isaiah 41:10, KJV

Clay glanced out of the upstairs sitting room window and caught sight of what appeared to be Gladdie's buggy coming up the lane, the horse trotting at a steady gait. But that didn't appear to be his Gladiola holding the reins. No, an elderly, plump woman was in command of the mare, which was definitely Gladdie's dapple gray swishing its tail as it pranced along. He frowned as the buggy wheels crunched on the gravel near the main entrance, just below the open window. Who might this be?

"I think we have some unexpected company." He turned to his sister and her friend, Miss Jacobs, each seated on a corner of the quilt he'd spread on the floor. A crew had begun laying some of the finished oak floorboards he'd ordered over the subflooring, but it was only partially complete. With the other two women present, this picnic wasn't turning out to be as romantic as he'd previously envisioned, but maybe his sister and her friend would retire for the afternoon once they'd eaten and he'd given them the promised tour of the interior of the mansion.

"That isn't Gladdie arriving?" Callie sipped some lemonade, her brow arching.

"No, not Gladdie. I'm not sure who it is," he said as the front door opened and closed, creaking each time. He really should ask the workers to oil those stiff new hinges.

A high-pitched voice called out from below, "Yoohoo! Anyone home?"

He crossed to the door. Should he go downstairs and greet this person? Perhaps a relation of Gladdie's if she was driving her buggy. But as he peeked out the sitting room door, the robust figure had already reached the top of the staircase. A mite spritely for someone of her size and age.

The lady yodeled again before turning to face the

front of the house. "Oh, there you are. You must be my niece's gentleman suitor, Clay."

"Hello..." He peered at her. "Yes, I'm Clay."

"My niece said you were a handsome gentleman. She certainly is head over heels in love with you, and now I can see why," the elderly creature gushed from under her hat.

Oh, another of Gladdie's aunts. She had a lot of those. Obviously, some he hadn't met. How could this lady find her way around with that hat blocking her view?

He grinned, however, unsure how to take this compliment. Was it true? Was Gladdie in love with him? It finally seemed possible again...especially given the way she had smiled at him after church when he'd mentioned kissing her.

The lady entered the sitting room and swept past him toward the quilt. "I'm Gladdie's Aunt Bertha. Just in from Atlanta. Ready for a cup of tea and some cakes after the journey I've had."

Clay suppressed a frown. Aunt Bertha? He'd never heard Gladdie mention an Aunt Bertha from Atlanta before. Something seemed off about this woman, but if this was Gladdie's aunt, he had better use his very best manners. "It's very nice to meet you."

The woman turned in a circle to take the room in. "My, how grand and spacious all of this is...much bigger than I expected. I mean, she told me it's still under construction."

He hurried to slide a crate over for her to sit on instead of the floor. "Please, make yourself as comfortable as possible. I haven't ordered the furniture yet."

"Oh, thank you. At my age, my bones do ache so after rattling around in a carriage, followed by a climb up a staircase." She sat down on the crate. "Now for those tea and cakes. And introductions."

"Hello." After handing Aurelia a plate, Callie leaned forward. "Would you care for a roast beef sandwich?"

"Nice to meet you." Aurelia smiled and nibbled some of the cold fried potatoes on her plate.

"And you as well. No to the sandwich, young lady, but thank you. I'm holding out for the tea and cakes my Gladdie promised Clay would have. And I'm really looking forward to a cup of steaming hot, properly steeped tea. You'd think one could get a decent cup of tea on a train these days, but of course, one cannot. In any case, my niece said she'd be along in a little while, but she didn't want to hold up the picnic."

"Tea and cakes?" He hadn't planned on tea and cakes. Had Gladdie really told her that, or had she misunderstood something? What had delayed Gladdie?

Aunt Bertha nodded. "Yes, Bergamot tea, she promised. And some of those sugary little finger cakes..." She paused to take a breath, her voice sounding a bit screechy and high.

Where was he going to get tea and cakes? Delia's cook had sent a crock of lemonade. He didn't even have teacups and saucers, let alone cakes. He'd offer lemonade, but he could tell it wasn't going to satisfy Bertha.

Aurelia's face took on a wistful expression. "I visited Atlanta once when I was a little girl. My grandmother lived on Meade Street, or perhaps it was Meade Avenue..." Then she looked down, her lips flattening. "But she passed away, and we were only there to pay our respects for her funeral."

"Oh, how dreadfully sad. I'm so sorry." Bertha sighed, and her heavy-looking hat tilted a little, but she straightened it.

Maybe he could get her mind off tea and cakes and funerals. "Gladdie didn't mention your arrival, but welcome to Kentucky. Traveling all that way from Atlanta must have been quite a journey." Clay scratched his head, cocking it to one side. Nor had Delia mentioned their aunt's arrival.

She nodded, pushing her glasses up. "It certainly is a long journey. A full week." Her voice wavered as if she was losing strength by the moment. "Which is why I'm looking forward to those cakes and tea."

Perhaps he shouldn't mention Atlanta or journeys...

Aunt Bertha snapped open a fan attached to her wrist and began waving it, releasing another long sigh. Another hint of how difficult the climb up the staircase had been for her after her harrowing train ride without a proper cup of tea? Not many trains ran on Sundays in Lexington. Perhaps the visit had been a surprise to Gladdie.

Maybe he should hurry across the street and ask Delia's cook for tea and cakes if that's what it would take to revive Bertha. It would only take a few minutes, after all. Then Gladdie could rest assured he'd taken good care of her elderly aunt. And perhaps he could take one of the roast beef sandwiches along with him.

Bertha swiveled her perch on the crate until she gazed directly at Miss Jacobs. "This pretty redhead must be your sister, Callie." Her voice crackled and wavered all over the place. Sometimes high pitched, sometimes lower pitched. Sometimes a bit scratchy. She turned toward Callie. "And this fair-headed, golden child must be her friend, Miss Aurelia."

Drat! He'd become so engrossed in figuring out who this aunt was that he'd forgotten to introduce his own sister and her companion, but Callie's laughter saved him.

"What a delightful mistake!" His sister sat upright. "I'm afraid you have us mixed up. I love that you think I'm a golden child, though. I'm his sister, Callie, and this is my companion and dear friend, Miss Aurelia. By the way, we have a Meade Avenue here in Lexington too."

"Yes, I'm Miss Aurelia Jacobs." Miss Jacobs raised her hand to her bodice. "But you can call me Aurelia. And speaking of Meade, isn't there someplace else that is quite known for the same name?" Her brows furrowed.

"You mean Belle-Meade plantation in Tennessee,

one of the finest thoroughbred farms in the South."
Aunt Bertha waved her fan.

Miss Jacobs brightened. "That's it!"

Aunt Bertha smiled. "Well, now that we have
remembered all of the Meade places, how sweet of you
all to include me in your lovely picnic. Yes, I'll have a
cup of that tea now…"

"And some of those cakes," Clay finished for her.
"I'll just make a quick dash across the street and get
some. Callie, if you could do whatever you can to make
Gladdie's aunt comfortable, I'll return as soon as I can."
He glanced at the sandwiches, debating the etiquette of
snatching one for the road.

Callie nodded, handing him an extra roast beef.
"Certainly. You can eat on the way. I'm sure you're
famished."

"Thank you." He grabbed the sandwich and dashed
for the door.

What if Delia's cook didn't have any cakes? He'd
figure something out. And maybe Gladdie would arrive
by the time he returned.

"Are you sure you won't have a roast beef
sandwich?" Callie arched her brow. "There
are plenty remaining. And some fried potatoes too."

Gladdie eyed the sandwiches on their plates while resituating her abundant rump on the crate. Her stomach was beginning to protest its emptiness. Now that her tea and cake request had served its purpose, removing Clay from the mix, she nodded. "Perhaps just one. And some of those potatoes. And my niece told me there might be some apple rhubarb pie. I'll have a slice of that."

"Oh, how nice that your appetite has returned now that you've had a moment to rest." Callie loaded the items onto a plate and handed it to her. "Here you are. Do tell us about your train journey. I just came to Lexington by train from the Richmond area, but it's a short ride unless you happen to purchase a ticket for the longer scenic route that stops in every small town along the way."

Gladdie remembered the long, scenic journey to Richmond all too well since Pa sometimes had done business there. Twenty-seven miles could take forever, especially in a slow, rumbling wagon. "My train ride? Oh yes. Hot, long, and miserable. It's a far piece from Alabama."

Aurelia narrowed her eyes. "I thought you just arrived from Atlanta."

Oh dear. Had she slipped up and said 'Alabama'? "Uh, that's because when we left my home in A-labama —yes, my other home in Alabama—we came through Atlanta. I have a home in both places." Gladdie lowered the hat some to keep some of her face covered and took a bite of her sandwich. She could barely open her mouth wide enough since the paint on her face had begun to harden into something akin to a thin plaster. And she should be more careful about things she said…

"You have two homes? How nice!" Aurelia sat up straighter.

Why not make Aunt Bertha exceedingly, abundantly rich? Perhaps they'd be more respectful and hand over that note all the sooner. "Actually, four. One in New Orleans, Louisiana. Another in Jackson, Mississippi. One in Mobile, Alabama. And one in Atlanta, Georgia. That one, Sherman nearly burned to the ground back in the day. I'm lucky to even be alive." Remembering to make her voice quake and waver wasn't easy given the hardening plaster. Much longer and her mouth would be permanently stuck open as if she were singing in the choir.

Callie's eyes widened. "You survived the Civil War?"

She nodded. The paint stuck to her face was beginning to itch and burn. "Such an ordeal, but we managed to hold on. Troops everywhere. Raids. Gunshots. Kidnappings."

"Kidnappings!" Aurelia breathed out the word like a dime novel enthusiast.

Gladdie murmured her assent. Enough about Atlanta. She had to find a way to get them on her side.

"Are you a Spencer aunt or a Lyndon aunt?" Callie

tilted her head to one side. "Delia is always talking about her Spencer aunts on her maternal side, and Colonel Lyndon on the paternal side of the family. He's like a hero around these parts."

Now what? Remembering a distant aunt by marriage to her father's brother who lived in Louisville, she shook her head. "Neither. I'm a Corkdale."

"A Corkdale?" Callie repeated.

"Well, I guess you could say I married into the Lyndons. Gladdie, Delia, and Veronica's father, Joseph Lyndon, has a brother, their Uncle James Lyndon. And he married Martha Corkdale, my other niece. Only we are quite estranged, you see. Martha has probably forgotten about me after all these years. The last time I saw her, she was only about the age of three. But there was a family rift. So I've sort of adopted Gladdie and her sisters as my great nieces. But it's been a great many years since I've seen any of them, and I thought it was high time. I have to decide which of my houses I'm going to give to each niece when I die."

"Ohh, I see. That makes sense." Callie finished the last bite of her sandwich. "I know all about family rifts. Say no more." She waved her hand.

Gladdie looked from one woman to the other. "In that case, you'll understand when I say I need your help, ladies."

"How can we help?" Aurelia set her plate aside.

"Well, to be perfectly honest, if I may count on you

to keep a secret, I really must stop my niece from marrying that nice gentleman, Clay. I don't want to hurt him, but I must see to it that she will marry..." Gladdie stared at the wall. "W-wal..ter! Yes, Walter." She took a nibble of her sandwich since the plaster wouldn't allow her to take a larger bite.

"Walter?" Aurelia's face lit up like the stars of heaven.

Gladdie nearly choked at her all-too-eager reaction. She recovered only because an urge to itch her face required all of her restraint. "Yes, Walter Wiggins."

"You don't say?" Aurelia cocked her head to one side and exchanged a glance with Callie.

"Who is Walter?" Callie leaned an ear toward her.

"It's a long story." Gladdie waved a gloved hand. "But he's perfect for my niece. I have my reasons. Far too many to concern you with today. Why, it'd take me until next week to tell you all of the reasons. But if she follows my wishes, I'll give her one of my houses. I have too many to take care of them all."

"Yes, four houses *is* a lot to keep up with." Aurelia nodded. "My mother can barely keep up with one, but it would be nice to have so many that I had to give some away."

"I really must convince my niece it's for the best, but we must break it to Clay gently, when we are sure his heart won't be broken. Just our secret for now..." Gladdie took another bite of her sandwich and glanced about. Could she get them to delay the idea of giving Clay that note?

Aurelia and Callie exchanged looks. Callie nodded toward the redhead. Maybe Gladdie's ploy was working. Her eyes widened as she tried a bite of the pie.

Aurelia flicked an imaginary speck of dust from the sleeve of her afternoon dress. "Well, I don't think you need to worry about her marrying Clay."

"Why is that?" Gladdie leaned forward. Would she finally mention that letter?

"We don't think we should tell Clay what we know just yet or how we came to know it. I mean, I've been waiting for the perfect moment to tell him. It really would break his heart. But if I had an aunt like you who cared about my future, I sure would appreciate such a kind benefactress." Aurelia hesitated. "We probably should share our secret with you..."

Her wistful tone and the fact that Delia had mentioned the young woman came from an impoverished background might have purchased Gladdie's sympathy...but for Aurelia's conniving ways. Something was amiss where Aurelia was concerned. Gladdie couldn't quite put her finger on it, but the way she'd laughed when reading Gladdie's note with Callie at the ball had been alarming.

Just as Gladdie held her breath in anticipation of the revelation, Aurelia's mouth twisted, and she clamped it shut. A bit more prompting was in order.

"What exactly makes you think my niece won't marry Clay?" Gladdie remembered to make her voice crinkle and tipped her hat a little lower to cover her face since the plaster felt as though it was beginning to crack. And it itched more than ever. "Please do put my fears to rest. Then I can stop pestering her about it and get her together with Walter all the sooner."

"The letter we found that she wrote him." Callie angled toward Aurelia. "Show her the letter, Aurelia."

Gladdie suppressed a sigh. So her suspicions had been correct all along.

Aurelia fished in her pockets. "I suppose it won't hurt anything at this point to let you see it for yourself, though I'd like it back once you've read it. It's our only proof that she doesn't love Callie's brother." She finally extracted the folded note and handed it over.

Gladdie resisted the urge to jump to her feet, instead accepting the letter graciously. Glancing down, pretending to read, she pushed Pa's spare reading glasses farther up on her nose. What options did she have now? Run? If she could tuck it down her décolletage and dart as fast as possible to the buggy... But they might chase her down and leave her with a lot of explaining to do to Clay.

Better to ask if she could hold onto it for a short while or offer to give it to Clay herself when the time was right. Or convince them that Gladdie should be forced to tell Clay the truth now. She needed to say something. She'd had enough time to read the letter twice over.

She sat up straighter. "What a relief! It seems she doesn't plan to marry him, after all. Perhaps the three of us can convince my niece to tell Clay sooner rather than later." Gladdie rose as fast as an old lady might. "If you'll wait right here, I'll go and get her."

But Aurelia jumped to her feet and snatched the letter from her hands before she could secure it on her person. "Go get her if you wish, but without this letter, how will I convince Clay that I'm the one who has been waiting for him all along?"

Gladdie gasped. Her intuition had been correct. Aurelia planned to steal Clay from her. She couldn't bear losing him again. He must never read that letter, especially since it wasn't even a true reflection of her feelings at this point. Had it taken her too long to come to this conclusion? Would she now lose him over this foolish incident? Had she thrown away her second chance with him?

Gladdie thought fast and mustered a placating and slightly condescending tone of voice. "I will give it to her as soon as I see her, my dear." She reached for the letter once more but could only grasp a corner of the paper as Aurelia pressed it to her chest. Gladdie pulled so hard that the corner tore off. In so doing, her voluminous skirt caught on the crate and she tumbled onto the floor, landing on her right side. Ugh! It was a hard landing, too, onto a finished portion of the floor. She lay still, recovering. At least she hadn't broken anything.

The door creaked open. Was that Clay returning? No! Could she pretend to have fainted?

~

"Aunt Bertha! What has happened here?" Clay's mouth dropped open as he took in Gladdie's elderly aunt sprawled on the floor and his sister and her companion staring at her, aghast.

Darting a glance at Clay, Aurelia flushed and took a step backward, attempting to stuff the paper she and Bertha had been fighting over into her skirt pocket. Was it a note of some sort? Why had she refused to share it?

As for Callie...he had trusted his sister to keep the peace for ten minutes, and she had failed him in this too.

Was Aunt Bertha injured? Someone had to help the lady, but where to set the tray of tea?

He slid it onto the crate and knelt to offer assistance. "How did you end up on the floor, Aunt Bertha?"

Gladdie's aunt rolled over, fluttering her lashes. "D-did you bring tea and cakes?"

"Yes, but you've given me quite a scare. You must have hit your head. Let me help you up." Obviously, the poor dear was addled by her fall.

Glaring toward Callie, he reached out to help the

elderly woman sit up, placing a hand on her shoulder and one on her forearm.

But such a squishy arm? And such a bony shoulder...

Her hat fell off as she scrambled to her feet, and her hair...it was lopsided? A wig?

He blinked. This wasn't Gladdie's Aunt Bertha. This was Gladdie in some sort of elaborate disguise, pretending to be an Aunt Bertha, if there even was such a person.

But why? Before he could outright ask her, she began talking rapidly in that elderly lady voice.

"Thank you for bringing the tea and cakes, but on second thought, I really must be going." She stared at Miss Jacobs, a crackle and waver in her voice. "I'm just plum worn out from the journey. I'll go and see what has become of our Gladdie."

He'd play along with Gladdie's ruse, but what was all of this about? "I think you'd better stay right here, Aunt *Bertha*." He held onto her arm quite firmly, causing her to look up at him with some alarm in her eyes.

She struggled to free herself, but his grip tightened just enough to hold her steady. Gladdie wasn't getting away that easily. Not until he figured this out.

He turned toward Aurelia. "Hand me that note you were just hiding."

Bertha covered her face with her hands as Aurelia handed the paper in question over. He gave it a shake to unfold it, along with a stern glance at Gladdie. How did his sister and Miss Jacobs still not see through her ruse?

He read the note while Gladdie hung her head.

He frowned. He'd expect a note of this nature from the woman he'd loved before the ball, but certainly not *after*. Especially not the woman he'd encountered earlier today, who'd seemed eager to have him kiss her and to tour the beautiful home they might one day share together.

"Clay, I can explain..." Gladdie's true voice filled the room.

Aurelia gasped. "You aren't Aunt Bertha!"

Callie covered her mouth. "Gladdie?"

Gladdie removed her hat and tossed it aside. Glaring at his sister with her hands on her artificially widened hips, she spouted, "Well I wouldn't have had to pretend to be someone else if you and Aurelia hadn't stolen my letter."

"Ladies, please." He kept his voice soft and turned to Gladdie. "Will you trust me to get to the bottom of this?"

She nodded, no longer resisting, crossing her arms over her chest. He released her.

Sighing, he turned to Aurelia. "Why did you have this? Where and when did you get it?"

"At the ball." Now it was Aurelia's turn to put her hands on her hips. "We were going to give it to you so you would know how Gladdie really feels about you. We didn't want to see you hurt."

Clay turned to Gladdie. "So this was written before the ball, *before* we talked."

Her emphatic nod confirmed it. "The letter must have dropped out of my purse, and I had decided not to give it to you when we talked after the ball. But it had gone missing during the dance. I suspected these two had taken it and were going to hold it over my head— hence, the creation of Aunt Bertha to get it back. I didn't want you to ever read it because it no longer applies to us."

Thank God! She cared about him. Her written words no longer applied. She'd said it herself. She... loved him?

He turned to his sister and her companion. "Callie, Aurelia, that was a terrible, rotten thing to do. It would have been more honorable of you to have returned the letter to its owner. You've placed Gladdie in a desperate situation, desperate enough to make up someone who doesn't even exist. Please, enough of all this. Kindly leave us."

Callie protested with a stomp of her foot. "But we were only thinking of you, and if you knew how much Aurelia cares about you..."

Clay pointed toward the door. "Out!"

Aurelia burst into tears, picked up her skirts, and fled.

"Now look what you've gone and done! Aurelia, wait!" Callie tossed her brother a harrumph and hurried after her friend.

Footsteps echoed from the staircase throughout the empty mansion. The front door creaked open and then closed. Finally, peace and quiet. He raked a hand through his hair as joy began to well up through his soul. Gladdie intended to give them a chance. Nothing could make him any happier.

"I'm sorry, Clay." She scratched her face. "I never meant for you to read that after we talked…"

"I know." He held his arms open as she fell into his embrace, both of them laughing. "But…Bertha?"

"It's all I could come up with to get that note back." She sighed, shaking her head at herself.

"You went to all of this trouble just so I would never read that letter?" He lifted a brow and she nodded.

"I couldn't bear losing you again." Gladdie swiped a tear from her eye.

"Don't cry. I'm not going anywhere. But I think you may have found your calling. To head up our theatrical department in our school for orphans."

She smiled up at him with misty eyes. "Do you mean it, Clay?"

"Of course I do. I really thought you were Aunt Bertha, until I felt all of the extra padding in your arm." He looked her voluminous figure over. "Your costume had me almost convinced."

She laughed again.

Things *had* changed since the ball. He'd overcome his pride issues and paranoia about the gossip that generally ensued anytime most folks learned about

Cora, enough to tell Gladdie the whole truth. And she had forgiven him, allowing him to put his arm around her in church. He could tell by the adoring and compassionate looks she'd been giving him too.

In fact, all he could imagine right now was her smiling at him from the buggy at church when he'd mention kissing her. He had no idea how that would go with all of that paint on her face...or what he was going to do with all of that tea and cake, but right now...

"Come with me." Grabbing her hand, he pulled her along.

They toured every room—the library, the drawing room, the music room, the kitchen, bedrooms, and a few rooms he wasn't sure what to do with. Perhaps a sewing room? A schoolroom?

Reaching the front door, he pulled her hand to his lips, brushing it with another kiss. "Plenty of room for the school you've always wanted for orphans right here...if you still want to become a teacher. Or you can be the director and we'll hire teachers."

She smiled, swiping some of the cracking paint from below her eyes. "Am I dreaming? It's all so beautiful, Clay."

"I know it's hard to picture without furnishings, flooring, wall coverings, wainscotting, and drapes, but..." He waved his hand. "I'd like you to help me choose all of it. And of course, we'll need some desks for the students. Any of the extra rooms would make a nice schoolroom."

"I can imagine how lovely it will be." She glanced up at where he imagined a chandelier dangling someday.

"Come and see the stables." He led her outside, where they explored the beginning of several barns, a carriage house, a tool shed, the chicken coop, the icehouse over the creek, and a long row of stables.

"English style. With cobblestones on the bottom and timber rafters. It's truly a dream..." She ran her hand along every stall as they explored the long, low building. None of them had doors yet, but they could imagine it.

"We'll fill these with horses to your heart's desire." He stopped in the middle of the stables and dropped down on bended knee. "Say you'll marry me..."

She was nodding, scratching more paint from her cheeks, trying to rearrange her pillows—lest they fall out of place, he supposed. Not very romantic. But he was only interested in her reply. "Yes, I'll marry you, Clay."

His smile widened to a grin. He laughed, wanting to pick her up and kiss her, pillows and all. Then he grew serious as he rose and drew her close.

"What?" She wore a puzzled expression, gazing up at him, mere inches from his lips.

"Shall we seal it with a kiss, Bertha?" He tried to keep a straight face but failed miserably, bursting into more laughter.

She glanced down as if just remembering her

plump, plaid-clad figure and chuckled, finally swiping the tilted wig off. She untucked her shirtwaist and yanked two pillows from under her well-padded walking suit. "Oh, you!"

Laughing, she pelted him with both pillows as he tried to escape—until he tripped on one of the pillows. Then she stumbled over him, both of them tumbling into the grassy area beyond the stable.

And then he kissed her...as if he'd fallen right into heaven.

CHAPTER SEVENTEEN

Doubt thou the stars are fire, Doubt the sun doth move,
Doubt truth to be a liar, but never doubt thy love.
—Shakespeare, *Hamlet*

Clay's kiss was gentle, tender, and passionate. "Have I told you how much I love you?" His blue eyes held her captive as he raised his brow.

"Not lately." She smiled.

"I love you this much." He spread his arms out as wide as they would go, making her laugh.

"Have I told you how much I love you?" She raised her own eyebrow to mirror his expression.

"Not lately." He grinned.

"This much!" She spread her arms as wide as she could.

He smiled.

"I need to wash this paint off my face." Gladdie scratched another chunk off. "I can't stop itching."

"Yes, you do, Bertha." He kissed her again, brushing her lips gently but lingering to return again with another soft sweep of his warm breath and tender lips.

It left her not only itching, but reeling and in a daze by the time he withdrew from the kiss. Gladdie had no remaining doubts left whatsoever about marrying the man. He had no intention of allowing Miss Aurelia Jacobs to squirm her way into their world. How silly to think he may have harbored any attraction for another woman when he only had eyes for her!

When her smile faded as she relaxed, staring up at the sky, he rested an elbow in the grass and leaned his head against his hand. "Callie and Aurelia, dealt with. House and grounds tour, mostly done. Wedding, agreed upon, and in the near future at a date, time, and place of your choosing, large or small. I'll let you pick out the biggest diamond in ten counties from the Lexington jeweler on Monday. Now, what other problems may I resolve for you today, Miss Gladys Lyndon?"

Relief rushed through her...to have someone in her corner she could trust. "Oh, Clay...all of our training clients have abandoned us at Velvet Brooks because they are in a panic, all except for Jake and Hercules." She rolled over onto her stomach, crossing her legs at her ankles, angled toward the sky, not caring where her skirts fell. She had far bigger problems—such as how to make payroll in April and May. "Where can Moon Lily race if Kentucky has no Phoenix Stakes and the Derby may not even happen? It's too late to register for the races at Latonia. I've missed the deadline for that, thinking there'd be a Phoenix. And now the Derby is up in arms too. How will I keep Velvet Brooks going without any local races? There are expenses and payroll for staff and all sorts of concerns. I don't know how Pa manages it all. Do you think Colonel Winn was serious about asking us to go to Europe to bring back those machines?"

"Yes, I do." He traced her nose with his index finger. "If there are no races here, then let's bring Kentucky and Moon Lily to Europe."

Did he mean it? Did he understand the enormity and complexity of what he was saying? She sat up and arranged her skirts to cover her ankles. "Are you quite sure about this? The registration fees will be sizeable. Hank and Red usually coordinate those things when they set up racing campaigns for our horses with Pa, but I can't bring myself to trouble him about it. Then there's the fare for passage across the Atlantic. And I'll need a chaperone. Not just any chaperone or a servant. Mother will insist upon someone who cares about us who is invested in watching out for us. Harvey won't qualify, mind you. And we'll have to speak to Red and Carter. Not to mention the decisions we'll have to make about who to take with us. I'll need Grace to style my hair and take care of my wardrobe. You know your sister will want to go even though this is supposed to be a mission we're on and not a tour, and she'll want to bring her companion. And we need to reunite you with your parents and reintroduce me to their lives before our wedding, and not ten minutes before." Gladdie finally paused to take a deep breath, and Clay chuckled.

She covered her mouth. "Oh dear. I'm sorry. I've dropped all of my burdens upon you all at once. You are so wonderful to listen to me go on like that without a single interruption."

"I've longed to hear you tell me the things on your heart and mind. These things are not too difficult. The children will stay here with their nanny. Callie and Aurelia are absolutely not going to Europe after the trouble they've caused. As for my parents, we can drive to Richmond in the Roadster and be there for dinner any evening this week. Tonight if you want..."

"Oh." Gladdie blinked. "I suppose there would be time for that." It seemed today would turn out to be even more eventful than she'd anticipated.

"We can speak to Red and Carter on Monday morning. I'm sure they'd love a chance to go to Europe. Don't forget Charlie. You'll need your best jockey. Then we'll call Colonel Winn and tell him we'll be in Paris in time for the Grand Prix de Paris, and afterwards to pick up those machines at Longchamp."

Gladdie sat up straighter. He really had it all figured out.

"Grace can begin packing for both of you on

Monday. Isn't she married to Carter? She'll be thrilled to accompany us. I'll book our passage according to Winn's instructions. I can write a bank draft to Red or Hank to cover the fees for the registration on Monday too. You can telephone your mother tomorrow and ask who she'd prefer as your chaperone. Don't forget Harvey. He wants the exclusive. We can plan our wedding when we return. Nothing to it." Clay snapped his fingers.

Were they really about to go to Europe? While they were there, might as well make the most of it. "Pa has always dreamed of winning the King's Vase at Ascot. May we please stop in London before Paris? Moon Lily is the worthiest horse of this chance from what we can tell, and I have you to thank for it."

"Not the Epsom?" He sat up, too, gathering her pillows.

She shrugged. "He'd like either one, but this year, the Epsom takes place much later than the King's Vase. There won't be time for Moon Lily to do that if we're going to make Longchamps and return in time for the Derby. Red can coordinate the European campaign, though. He'll know what to do."

"Correct me if I'm wrong, but you'd like Moon Lily to have a shot at Ascot and at Longchamps?"

She held her breath and nodded.

"Fine with me. Tell Red to make it happen, and I'll pay the registration fees." He rose and pulled her to her feet.

She threw her arms around his neck. "Thank you, Clay!" Now that they were engaged, she could accept such a generous gift. As his wife, a whole new world would surely open up to her. Not to mention, her dowry would be a considerable sum...not that a man of his means would truly need it, but at least she would not come to the marriage emptyhanded.

"Now, let's get you home to wash up before your face turns red."

"Then a drive to Richmond for dinner this evening?" She peeked up at him as they headed toward her buggy.

"I'll have to wear my boater hat so mother can see I've come into some fashion sense, but if you so desire..."

"I do." Swiping away more paint flaking from her cheeks, she smiled with contentment in her heart. He had solved all of her problems and answered questions she'd been grappling with for weeks. Her fears began to disappear.

RICHMOND, KENTUCKY

Two hours after the tour of Hickory Chase, Clay held Gladdie's hand as he knocked on the door of Amber Hall. They were on the outskirts of Richmond, the house nestled deep in the countryside. He'd never laid eyes on it before. Trees hid most of the property, but they had a great big front lawn and a long drive. He turned around on the stone veranda to inspect everything and fussed with his tie, ensuring it was tucked properly into his sweater vest.

"Do you think your parents and Cora will remember me?" Gladdie smoothed the front of her pale-yellow evening dress and adjusted the matching hat perched on her brunette locks.

"I'm sure they will." He gave her gloved hand a gentle squeeze. He had questions too. Would Otto treat him with respect? Would Cora have one of her episodes and embarrass him in front of his fiancée?

A few seconds passed before the front door swung open wide. There stood his mother with her mouth agape and shock in her wide eyes. About the same stature as Gladdie, Ma had always been petite, except now she carried a few extra pounds. Were those endearing crow's feet and a few strands of gray in her dark hair because of Cora...or just the passage of time?

"Clay, is that you?" She nearly barreled into him for an embrace, clearly hardly able to contain her joy. Burying her face in his chest, she sobbed. "You've come home at last."

"It's so good to see you, Ma." When she pulled away to have another look at him, he offered a sheepish grin. Tugging Gladdie in close to his side, he asked, "You remember Gladdie, don't you?"

"Gladdie! Yes, of course. So lovely to see you again." She stepped back and gestured behind her. "Please, come inside. We were going to have dinner soon, but I'll have the cook set two more plates. I hope you both love chicken and dumplings. There's a blackberry cobbler for dessert too."

"That sounds delicious. Thank you." Gladdie exchanged a smile with him as she stepped across the threshold.

Tears brimmed in his eyes, but joy swelled in his heart. His mother's smile told him they'd done the right thing in making the visit. As Gladdie had put it on the way there, how could they set sail for Europe unless things were resolved with his family?

"I can hardly believe you are here..." Ma reached for his hand. "Let me just have a quick word with Cook for some tea and setting extra plates at the table. Then I'll take you to see Otto in the parlor. He'll be so happy to see you, both of you. Please, make yourselves comfortable." She waved toward a hall table and a small cloak room where Gladdie could remove her hat and shawl.

He nodded, and his mother disappeared down the spacious hall toward the kitchen. Amber Hall was as nice as his mother had described it in her letters. A fine country house with elegant furnishings. Nicer than any home his parents had ever had before.

Ma soon returned and led them to the parlor, where her short, stocky husband now snored after having drifted off to sleep while reading—as evidenced by the book which now lay face down across his chest. When Ma shook his arm, his eyes popped open.

He swung his feet off the footrest and jumped up from his chair, blinking. "Clay?" His face lit up with a wide grin. "How marvelous that you have come to visit us! How have you been? Please, come in. Come sit down with us." He gestured toward the rest of the room. "Who is this beauty at your side?"

Ma spoke before Clay could as she took the seat beside his stepfather. "You remember Miss Gladys Lyndon—Gladdie, from Velvet Brooks—don't you, Otto?"

Otto set his book aside and nodded vigorously. "Oh, yes, of course. How nice to see you again, Miss Lyndon. Please, feel at home. I must have dozed off. Such a pleasant Sunday afternoon. Quiet out here in the countryside."

"Thank you and likewise, but you can call me Gladdie," she said as they settled onto the sofa across from his parents.

His mother brightened, another warm smile spreading across her face. "And please, call us Eula and Otto."

A uniformed servant appeared with a tea tray and placed it beside his mother, then took her leave. While Ma poured, Clay assessed the pleasant space, taking note of the staff's efficiency and the excellent condition of the upholstery, drapes, and flooring. His family seemed well taken care of and happy, and for this he was glad.

Before Ma could pass Otto a cup of tea, he held up his finger, then went to a desk at the far end of the room and opened a drawer. He returned with two packages he placed in Clay's hands. "This is a train for Emery. And this is a doll for Olympia. Birthday gifts. We didn't know where to send them when you left New York."

Clay's brows rose. "You didn't have to…"

"No, I wanted to. We wanted to." Otto glanced at Ma, who nodded. "We're so hopeful to meet them now that you're in Kentucky again."

"He picked them out himself. I only wrapped them," Clay's mother explained.

"I'll bring the children next time," Clay promised, making their faces light up. "And Gladdie and I have some happy news to share. We're engaged to be married. We haven't set a date yet, but we'd love for you all to be there on our special day, sometime after we return from Europe."

"Oh, my goodness!" Ma beamed. "That is happy news, indeed. And a trip to Europe…did you hear that, Otto?" She raised her voice, leaning closer to his stepfather. "They are engaged to be married and going on a trip to Europe, but we'll be invited to the wedding." She faced him and Gladdie again with a subtle wink. "He's a little hard of hearing at times."

"Congratulations! How exciting…" Otto's face lit up, his eyes widening. "We are very happy for you."

Ma beamed with her hands folded in her lap. "Will the wedding take place in Lexington?"

Clay turned toward his fiancée—strange and wonderful to think of her as such—and she nodded, answering for them. "Yes, at my home church. Mama will insist it's there."

"I'm absolutely delighted." Ma smiled warmly before sipping some of her tea. "I can't wait to hear more about it."

Clay covered Gladdie's hand with his and gave hers a gentle squeeze. He turned back to his parents. "How is Cora?"

"The nurse should bring her over from her house for dinner any minute now." Lowering her voice, his mother added, "She had a bad night last night. Escaped to the meadow in the middle of the night, dancing away, carrying on, hollering at the trees. The nurse had fallen asleep. It's hard for the staff to stay awake all night sometimes, you know. So Cora has been resting today."

"I see. I'm sorry to hear that." Clay leaned forward. "Does that happen often?"

"No, but about once every few months or so..." Otto shrugged. "She gets restless. We don't get much company, you see. But it's for the best. We've tried to socialize her in the past, and it never works out for long. The episodes increase."

Clay nodded. "How does she seem, otherwise? Has she improved at all?"

Ma tilted her head to one side. "She is happy,

although she has good days and bad days, as we have told you in our letters. She likes it better than that awful place in Lexington."

"What does she do with her time?" He had received a few letters from Cora over the years, but it would be nice to hear the answer from his parents.

"Oh…" His mother gestured with both hands. ""She does a lot of embroidery. Loves to draw pictures in her sketchbook. All kinds of things. She sketches leaves and flowers, houses, whatever she puts her mind to. Butterflies. She reads sometimes. She loves to play with her cat. She named it Archie."

"You'll tell me if she needs anything, if you and Otto need anything…won't you?" Clay glanced from Otto to Ma.

They nodded, but it was Otto who spoke up. "We are well provided for here, Clay, thanks to you. We would never complain about a single thing, but if we did need something, yes, we'll tell you."

"Good. I'm glad." Clay turned toward her. "Why don't we show Gladdie the garden? You said you have a little flower garden out back?"

"Oh, yes. The lilies are all in bloom. We love to sit outside and read or relax there." Ma smiled and rose. "Follow me."

Otto came, too, and soon they were all laughing and talking about old times, remembering baseball games and church picnics, admiring his mother's pleasant flower garden behind the two-story, Georgian-style country house with its symmetrical windows and stone front. As they sat on some benches, Clay couldn't help staring at the guest house, a short distance from the garden, where Cora resided.

"Would you like to tour Cora's home?" Ma's brow arched.

Clay shook his head. "Perhaps the next time, when we can stay longer. It's nice to imagine where she is, and that she's in a safe place with good care."

"Yes, it certainly is. And we have you to thank for that, son." His mother reached for her husband's hand. "Don't we, Otto?"

His stepfather dipped his chin. "Yes, yes, we do. We'll never forget all you've done for our family, Clay. We are very aware of that and pray for God's blessings on you each day."

Their words warmed his heart as he chanced a glance at Gladdie, who smiled at him with misted eyes. The sacrifices he'd made had not gone unnoticed. Perhaps they would never know all that it had cost him and his fiancée, but hearing them now stirred his heart with all sorts of positive emotion. They'd thanked him over the years in their letters, of course, but something about hearing their words of appreciation aloud gave him resolution and encouragement.

At dinnertime, as his mother said, a uniformed nurse brought Cora into the dining room, leading her by the hand as if Cora were a child. The nurse wore a look of surprise to see guests in the house, but she simply nodded and left after ensuring her charge was ready to be seated with the family.

When Cora's gaze fell on Clay and Gladdie already seated at the table, the young woman stopped short of her seat and stared at him. His sister buried her face in her hands. Clay rose to go around and hug her, but before he could embrace her, she burst into tears. He lingered like a lost sheep, not knowing what to do to console her.

"You been gone too long, Clay Grinstead!" Cora stood back from him, wagging her finger.

He spread his arms wide, and when she moved forward, gave her a long hug. "I've missed you, Cora."

After he released her, she swatted his shoulder playfully, swiping tears away with her other hand. "Missed you too."

Dabbing the corner of her eyes with a handkerchief, Gladdie stepped up to greet Cora.

"Cora, do you remember Gladdie?" He pulled Gladdie to his side. "We're getting married soon."

Cora stared at her with her head tilted to one side, a strange look in her eyes. As if she couldn't decide whether to trust Gladdie or not.

Gladdie smiled. "Hello, Cora. It's so nice to see you again."

There was a long pause, and he held his breath. Best to take it slow, so Clay placed a hand over Gladdie's while they waited for a response. Otto and his mother did not interrupt, apparently preferring to allow things to unfold naturally, for which he was grateful.

Had Cora pushed all memories of her time at finishing school with Gladdie and Callie away?

"Nice to see you, too," she finally said. "Let's eat. I'm hungry. You pray, Clay."

The meal progressed nicely. Conversation centered around the progress at Hickory Chase, and occasionally, a remark came from Cora about her latest drawing or embroidery project. Otto asked about Gladdie's family and the horses at Velvet Brooks, and she shared about them all, including their plans for Moon Lily. Clay gave them an update about Callie, sparing them an account of her latest antics. They laughed and laughed about Callie driving into Gladdie's fence. Thankfully, Gladdie laughed too. Ma kept reaching out to squeeze his hand.

When dinner ended, Clay insisted they had to head back before dark. Cora asked them to wait while she ran to fetch something. When she returned a few minutes later, they all gathered on the narrow front veranda to say their goodbyes.

Ma rested a hand on Gladdie's shoulder. "My son has always loved you, Gladdie. I've prayed for a long time that someday it would all come out right. I'm so happy for you two."

"Thank you, Eula. That fills me with peace and joy. As my mother has said, some things take time to work out."

"I'd like you to have these." Cora pushed a few of her sketching books into Clay's hands.

"Thank you, Cora. That's very thoughtful of you." He gave her a big bear hug. "I'll see you again soon. Listen to Ma and Otto."

She harrumphed. "I'll try."

"Will you send postcards from Europe?" Ma clutched a shawl to her shoulders.

"We will," Clay promised. Unlike some folks, sending correspondence was something he enjoyed. "I'm sure Gladdie will help me remember." And she was already consenting with vigorous nodding.

"It's so nice to see you both. Please come back soon." Otto seized Clay's hand with both of his. He gave it a hearty squeeze, then he pulled Clay into a hug and reached up to clap him on the back.

"We will definitely come back soon." Gladdie embraced each of his parents and Cora along with her promise.

"You have the gifts for the children?" Otto asked for the second time.

"Right here under my arm." Clay showed him the presents.

"Good, good." Otto smiled with approval in his eyes.

Clay helped Gladdie into the Roadster, and they waved while his mother wiped tears from her eyes.

Gladdie held up a butterfly sketch as he sped along on the country roads. "Look at how detailed and beautiful these drawings are. They're so lifelike. Can we frame a few for Hickory Chase?"

He stole glances at what she showed him. "I'd like that."

And he loved the way his fiancée had brought him back together with his family.

~

As far as Gladdie could tell, the visit couldn't have gone better, but did her fiancé agree? After a while, she angled toward him as the breeze ruffled through their hair. "Penny for your thoughts."

He kept his eyes on the road, the round headlights illuminating the dusky path. "It was good to see my mother and sister. I can't even tell you how much joy it brought my soul." He released a long sigh.

She fixed her gaze on the road for a moment. "Family is family. We have to support and love each other, in good times and bad. Cora is a dear and wounded soul, deserving all the love, support, and emotional stability we can give."

"I couldn't have said it any better." He glanced at her. "You know, I once wondered if I could ever forgive Otto. And I have done so to the best of my ability, time and time again. But tonight, I experienced a completely different man, and one who is much easier to forgive. One who was sorry for the way he behaved, far humbler, and doing everything he could to make up for it. Life is messy, but tonight, it's also very good. Is our Heavenly Father smiling down on us, Gladdie?"

She reached over and squeezed his hand, her heart bursting with joy. "I'm sure He is. Tonight was a true gift from above."

What other gifts did their Heavenly Father have in store? She could hardly wait to find out.

CHAPTER EIGHTEEN

In their (horses') eyes shine stars of wisdom and
courage to guide men to the heavens.
—Herman Melville, American novelist

MARCH 26, 1908

Gladdie could hardly contain her enthusiasm
when the Thursday of their departure for
Europe arrived. Clay kept her hand tucked into the
crook of his arm during the hustle and bustle at the
train station while attendants loaded their trunks. The
locomotive would transport them to New York, where
Aunt Mae would join the expedition—in accordance
with Gladdie's mother's wishes, as Gladdie had
suspected. And Clay had asked her pa over the tele-

phone for his permission to marry her, to which Pa had given a resounding yes. Now he could read about their journey in the newspapers with an expectation of a successful outcome all the way around.

The scents of coal, hot steam, and oil wafted under her nose as they said their farewells to family and friends. A shrill whistle released, signifying boarding time, along with a train master's call, "All aboard!" Yet another billow of steam puffed a cloud across the walkway, and frequent clanking from the train rose to their ears.

Passengers hurried to step on and find their seats or compartments while families clustered about, hugging travelers or waving goodbye. A young boy tried to sell copies of the *Lexington Gazette*, and another offered to shine shoes for gentlemen on their way to Main Street. A mother hurried after her husband, pulling her wide-eyed and teary daughter along while carrying an infant sleeping through all of the commotion.

Among those sending off other travelers were their family members and friends, Jake and Delia, Delia's four girls, Ollie and Emery with their nanny, and Gladdie's four grandparents and two aunts. Callie and Aurelia seemed to have recovered from their disappointments. They now waited alongside a railing with Mary Lou Sullivan after wishing them well.

Nearly all of the Velvet Brooks staff had turned up, too, all waiting patiently to wave them off while Gladdie and Clay spoke to Colonel Winn. It seemed half of the town had read Harvey's first newspaper article about the expedition, and even some townsfolk milled about, eager to wish them and their racing team—Red, Carter, and Charlie—a cheerful send-off.

Harvey and his photojournalist, a fellow by the name of Roger Smith, set up equipment to take a photograph of their departure. Gladdie was particularly glad she'd settled on wearing the best of her two traveling suits, a dark-plum ensemble and matching hat with netting which Delia had trimmed.

Colonel Winn had met her and Clay at the train station prior to their scheduled boarding time, a long narrow box in his hands. He handed it to Clay with an envelope.

"What's this?" Clay's brows furrowed.

Colonel Winn grinned, tapping the box. "The finest Kentucky bourbon for Jean-Claude, and a bank draft made out to him for the cost of the machines. The other bank draft is made out to you, Clay, to cover the cost of your journey, as we discussed. There'll be a bonus for you and Gladdie when you return, as well as the best seats in the house for this year's Derby. Ask for Pierre at the entrance gate to Longchamps. He's a concierge assigned to lead you to a fine seat in the clubhouse for the race, but only give the box and bank draft directly to Jean-Claude after the race. He'll give you a steamer trunk with the three totalizer machines inside."

Clay offered a dutiful nod. "Thank you, sir. I'll see to it personally."

"We'll do our best not to let everyone down." The pressure was on, but she didn't mind. The task seemed easy enough with Clay at her side. And any stress paled in comparison to her excitement about the adventure ahead of them.

"All my best to Moon Lily," Colonel Winn said.

How kind of the colonel to be thinking about Moon Lily winning races when he had so many things on his mind to save the Derby. "Thank you. Our crew boarded our champion a little while ago, and I can only pray she travels well and shows Europe a taste of what we Kentuckians do best."

Her remark drew a wide smile from Colonel Winn and her fiancé.

Almost afraid to ask, she tilted her head. "Have you found the other machines yet?"

His mouth twisted to one side, and his chin dipped. "No, but we're still looking. Unfortunately, our second search of Clark's home turned up empty. I'm still confident we'll find them. And we've got those mechanics on standby in case they're in poor shape."

She nodded. "Clay and I are praying for a miracle."

"So am I, Gladdie." Colonel Winn squeezed her hand and winked at them. "Have a safe journey. We'll see you soon. Go win some races and bring us back those machines from Paris..."

Harvey called out, "Time for a pose!"

She beckoned Red, Carter, and Charlie to join Colonel Winn, Clay, and herself by the train steps for the photograph. After all, their crew would be doing most of the heavy lifting. They all squeezed together and held still, smiling as Harvey bade them while Roger memorialized the moment for Harvey's syndicated column. Then Harvey and his one-man crew hurried to gather their equipment and follow them onto the train.

The trunks were loaded. Grace herded them up the steps like a cattle boss. Gladdie couldn't deny her excitement as she waved one last time to their family and friends from the windows of the private compartment she would share with Grace. Clay, Red, Carter, and Charlie crowded inside to wave out of the windows alongside them, but the men would have their own compartment next door.

They would arrive in New York in three days for a whirlwind shopping spree for her trousseau with Aunt Mae, after which they'd set sail from New York's harbor for England. The whistle blew and the train began to chug. And they were off!

APRIL 2, 1908
DEPARTING NEW YORK CITY

"Are you sure Moon Lily will be all right?" Gladdie eyed the stables below deck in the hold near the front of the Cunard Line's *Queen Mary* a few hours after the ship had set sail.

They'd settled into their cabin suites and unpacked, but she had to be sure Moon Lily was comfortable. "Those stalls seem awfully small."

"They are, but everything is padded for the horse's safety." Clay also pointed to the wide cloth strapped under the filly's belly. "She has extra support, too, for the duration of the journey. Red, Carter, and Charlie can check on her every day, multiple times each day. They are given hay, oats, water, and it's a nice break from their usual routine."

"If you say so." She eyed the horse one last time and patted her nose before they headed to the upper deck to have a look around.

He tucked her hand into the crook of his elbow as they climbed a narrow staircase with just enough room for them to walk side-by-side. "She'll have sea legs when we reach England, but Red will work with her for a week or so to get her ready for the race. They have it well in hand. You'll need to show Red and his crew that you trust their expertise."

She sighed. "I suppose you're right. I'm just a little surprised at how horses are confined to those stalls. Though it does seem as if we aren't the only ones heading to Europe for horseracing from America. The ship's stable is full, and we've already met two other prominent families on board from Kentucky."

Clay nodded. "It confirms to me that we've made the right decision to bring Moon Lily to Europe for a chance to race."

As they strolled, he explained all of the reasons the horses could not exercise on the same decks with the passengers. Apparently, he'd been talking to Red, learning things from him. What if a horse jumped overboard or began kicking, damaging the ship or injuring someone else? Clay pointed out all of the reasons, and they did make sense.

She would have to become accustomed to the idea of the horses being trapped below deck for nearly a week while they crossed the Atlantic.

When they joined Aunt Mae after their stroll around the upper deck, the older lady with her perfectly coiffed silvery white hair looked up from reading and patted the lounge chair next to her. Gladdie settled into the chaise, and Clay took the one beside hers. Aunt Mae smiled indulgently at them. "This makes for a refreshing change of pace, does it not? I must say, of all my nieces, you are the one I would choose to accompany to Europe, my dear Gladdie."

Gladdie smiled, lifting her brows. "Why is that?"

"Well, for one, you're so easy to shop for. You're not nearly as fussy as Veronica and Delia were about your trousseau. You found your wedding dress pattern on the first day in New York. With Veronica, I had to constantly look over my shoulder because of her future relations causing all sorts of chaos. And with Delia, who couldn't make up her mind about her suitors, your pa and I had to endure a harrowing carriage ride to retrieve a stolen horse!"

Gladdie couldn't help but chuckle. She'd had plenty of drama in her life, but thankfully, Aunt Mae hadn't been there to witness it.

Her aunt continued, shifting in her lounger. "No, the two of you have it all together. You are happily engaged. Your home is being built in Kentucky. You know where you're getting married. All you have to do is set a date and order the invitations when you return from Europe. You do have an annoying photographer and an awkward journalist following us around, but I'll still supremely enjoy my time with you. I just hope you don't intend to do too much sneaking around to kiss each other, because I could easily fall asleep every afternoon on these chaise lounges."

Gladdie and Clay exchanged glances, and unavoidable smiles spread on their faces. She couldn't pass up the chance to tease him. "Sneaking around to kiss? Not my fiancé. He isn't the sneaking around type. Clay likes to scandalize folks by kissing me in public whenever possible. Isn't that right, darling?" While she jested, what she'd said wasn't far from the truth.

He drew her hand to his lips and brushed the back of it with his lips to prove her point. Then he grinned. "She knows me well."

Aunt Mae shook her head, but she was laughing and wore a wide grin. "I can see this is going to be a fun journey with you two lovebirds. And a peaceful voyage, since you've not brought any relations along to disturb us."

Why did her sisters seem to think their aunt was so strict? So far, the sweet, fun lady before her hadn't given her any rules except for a midnight curfew. Grace, on the other hand, would keep her on her toes.

But yes, the lack of family drama should help keep the voyage peaceful. Gladdie made a little face. "I confess, Aunt Mae, I'm the one who wanted to bring Clay's children along, and I didn't think we could say no to his sister and her companion. As I feared, they did beg us to come. But Clay put his foot down, and now I think he made the right decision." She turned toward Clay and smiled. "I guess we've learned to put ourselves first for a change, and we've learned the hard way, by years of sacrifice in being apart, haven't we, darling?"

"You can say that again." He rolled his eyes. Then he patted Gladdie's hand. "We certainly have lots of time to make up for, and I intend to guarantee we have a marvelous time on this adventure."

Aunt Mae clucked her tongue. "I approve. And it sounds as though you've done the right thing by leaving some folks at home so you can have some time to yourselves. Keep doing that throughout your marriage and it will be a lasting one."

Gladdie couldn't help but smile at the thought of becoming Mrs. Clay Grinstead as she turned her gaze to the endless miles of ocean, but she needed to ensure the future of her family's farm before she could fully embrace her own.

~

On a brilliant Saturday near Windsor Castle, Gladdie squeezed her eyes shut. She could hardly believe the day of Moon Lily's debut had finally arrived. The gunshot reverberated into the air, and the horses were off on the turf. Not a dirt track like those at home.

She'd felt like Queen Victoria herself, staying at Claridge's on 51 Brook Street in London. The hotel had columns in the foyer, a giant ballroom, and an impressive chandelier made of gold with crystals from Austria. The biggest she'd ever seen. Their suite had a lavish sitting room too.

Clay had rented a driver and motor carriage to take them to a few museums and other fascinating sites. The Victoria and Albert Museum had been Gladdie's favorite, but it had been equally enthralling to tour the state rooms at Kensington Palace, peer up at Westminster Abbey's enormous ceiling, and stand in the courtyard at Windsor Castle.

When the robust figure of King Edward—the seventh King Edward, if memory served—appeared at the racing event, she had to pinch herself. It all seemed so surreal. She could hardly wait to tell Pa all about every detail of her travels.

Servants for the royals had set up a picnic tent with linen-covered tables and chairs for the king and a few of his friends instead of his customary box, as she discovered from new acquaintances who spoke mainly to her aunt from a neighboring picnic blanket. They said the king's tent was due to the organizers declaring the day's events a picnic racing day. Thus, all of the onlookers had brought picnic baskets and blankets to sit on. Clay had inquired at the hotel about the arrangements, and they had accommodated them with a quilt and a basket stuffed with all sorts of delectable foods.

Since Queen Victoria's son had commissioned the coveted vase, it was a popular race drawing a large crowd spread out on the lawn surrounding the track. Not to mention, the generous purse to accompany the prize. More than enough to secure Velvet Brooks for the next few years if Moon Lily became the victor.

When the race began, she held a pair of elegant binoculars made with a mother of pearl covering and gold trim to her eyes—an extravagant gift from Clay, and perfect for the opera outing they planned for their last night in England. Barely breathing as the horses flew around the track, she followed every stride Moon Lily made as she and Charlie raced in the opposite direction around the oval—a clockwise run as opposed to the counterclockwise run in America. She suppressed a laugh at the way the British jockeys sat upright astride their horses, while the handful of American jockeys leaned low over the manes. Could Charlie and Moon Lily bring home that vase for Pa?

As the race continued, Gladdie wasn't the only one who couldn't remain sitting on her quilt. Even Aunt Mae stood alongside her and Clay at the railing, peering through her lorgnettes to better view the competition.

A horse tried to edge in front of Moon Lily and crowd her out, but their mare's nostrils flared and the filly took off, moving into the lead. She held her position for the rest of the race as Charlie leaned low over her mane, finally riding across the finish line a furlong ahead of the other horses. Over the course of one mile, six furlongs, and thirty-four yards to complete the race, the filly had made her mark on England. Gladdie cheered, her heart soaring. Of course, Moon Lily had won. Had they ever doubted the possibility, for even a minute? All of her training races proved she could.

The crowd clapped, and Charlie bounced along astride the filly toward the winner's circle where Gladdie, Clay, Aunt Mae, Red, Charlie, Carter, and even Grace hurried to meet Harvey and his photographer as they accepted the King's Vase. There, Gladdie and her team held up the vase for Pa to see it in a photograph from Chesapeake Manor when he read the newspaper. She'd bring the prize home to display at Velvet Brooks.

After another short voyage and a train ride to Paris, they checked into Le Meurice, one of the oldest hotels in the 1st arrondissement of Paris, on the edge of the Tuileries Garden along the Seine River. Gladdie thoroughly enjoyed her suite of rooms she shared with Aunt Mae and Grace. Clay, Red, Carter, and Charlie had a neighboring suite, just as they'd had in London.

On their first night in Paris, Clay took her and Aunt Mae to dine at the hotel's rooftop garden restaurant under the canvas of a spectacular sunset, the serenade of a symphony, and a view of the city that went on for miles. They feasted on a steak dinner and then rode in a carriage to see the Eiffel Tower.

The city lit up at night all around the iron landmark. Parisians and tourists rode past on bicycles, strolled by with their friends, and huddled close together in couples. Harvey followed them at a distance, ever on the lookout to record the ambience of the setting. He urged them to pose while Roger captured their photograph against the backdrop of the tower. Clay pulled Gladdie close and kissed her for the picture, making her and Aunt Mae laugh.

"Now our love has been captured for the whole world to see," he said, tucking her closer to his side.

"I'm glad." She tilted her head. "Harvey said our engagement is part of what makes the story interesting

to his readers. I guess they're rooting for us to succeed."
She'd been reading each of his newspaper articles
documenting their progress toward saving the
Kentucky Derby.

"Shall we stroll along the Seine? Or would you like
to ride in one of those steamer yachts or perhaps one of
the boats offering dinner and dancing to see the sites
along the riverbanks?" He pointed to a luxury steamer
yacht passing a slower, larger riverboat with a big
paddle wheel churning the water.

"I'd prefer a romantic stroll along the river. And I
think Aunt Mae, Grace, and I would enjoy stopping to
explore the booths of vendors selling all of those books,
trinkets, and sweet little paintings of Paris. I want to
pick something out for Ollie and Emery."

"Sure. Fine with me."

After perusing some of the booths, Gladdie found a
small painting of Notre Dame and a bracelet for Ollie
and a miniature replica of the Eiffel Tower and a
painting of the Seine for Emery. She also purchased
postcards to write notes to their family and friends.
She'd wrap the gifts for the children with the items
she'd found for them in England...a trinket box for
Ollie and a toy soldier for Emery. She'd also selected
British tea for other family members and friends.

Clay eyed the little treasures she'd found with an
approving sparkle in his blue eyes. "You've taken to
being a mother so naturally."

She dipped her chin. "I miss them already, and I

can't wait to see their faces when they open their gifts. I'm looking forward to getting to know them better when we return."

They visited the Louvre the next day, which took most of the day. Notre Dame, the day after that. The charming architecture of the city stunned her. Every roof had an elaborate design.

The last morning before the race, they enjoyed sitting in the sunshine outside a French café to sip coffee and watch Parisians feed the pigeons or hurry past on their way somewhere.

On event day, Saturday, May 9, all sorts of ladies and gentlemen wearing the latest fashions arrived at Longchamps. The track was nestled inside city limits but close to the river winding through Paris. After navigating them through heavy traffic which seemed to bottleneck everywhere, the carriage driver Clay had hired came to a stop near the main gate.

As Clay, Gladdie, and Aunt Mae climbed down from the carriage with Clay's assistance and made their way to the entrance, a great number of yachts also carried racing enthusiasts along the river toward the course. To Gladdie's relief, trees encircled much of the racecourse, blocking the cityscape and providing the ambience of a large park, though roofs and a few taller buildings peeked over the treetops.

Gladdie and Aunt Mae had greatly enjoyed purchasing hats to wear to the race, and their new creations perched atop their heads. Why did a new hat always put a smile on her face? And today even more so, for Moon Lily would show Paris she was full of spirit, stamina, and speed. And then, by picking up those machines from Jean-Claude, they would save the Kentucky Derby.

"Remember what Colonel Winn said. We're supposed to ask for a concierge named Pierre who will lead us to excellent seating in the clubhouse," Clay reminded her and Aunt Mae as they approached the row of clerks granting entrance to those who purchased a ticket. They had made excellent progress despite the abundance of attendees heading in the same direction. He clutched the box for Jean-Claude under one arm. "And he'll see to it that we have anything else we need."

"How nice." Aunt Mae lifted her skirts with one hand, doing her best to keep up. She held onto Gladdie's arm, and Gladdie held onto Clay's arm. "I may enjoy this as much as that picnic race at Ascot."

Coming from a woman who did not particularly like horseracing because of the evils of those who gambled excessively, this remark rendered Gladdie speechless for a moment. But she nodded, taking in the racing fans purchasing tickets from the clerks ahead of them. "Feast your eyes on all of the fashions, Aunt Mae. Victoria and Delia would love this."

The gentlemen wore top hats, bowler hats, and boater hats. Some dressed in suits and others in more casual styles. Ladies wore their finest hats, afternoon dresses, and walking suits.

"They surely would. Look at how short those dresses are, though. The ladies are showing their ankles." Aunt Mae's eyes nearly popped out of her head.

Gladdie chuckled, spotting Harvey and Roger bustling through the crowd to catch up with them, since they'd taken a different mode of transportation with more room for their equipment.

The men reached them, breathless. She and her aunt greeted them while Clay purchased tickets and mentioned Pierre's name to the clerk, who stepped away momentarily to find the concierge.

In short order, Pierre, a tall, dark-haired gentleman, appeared through an office door with the clerk. He came around the counter to shake hands with each of them. "Bonjour! Welcome to Longchamps, *mes amis*. Jean-Claude told me you would be here. Please, follow *moi*. I take you to one of the best tables in the clubhouse." He uttered the words in a heavy French accent, motioning them with an extended arm and a pleasant smile.

They hurried along after Pierre, parting company with those purchasing general admission who headed down a passage toward the stands as they followed their guide to the double doors of the clubhouse he held open for them.

Inside, they climbed a few steps and crossed a wide landing, where Pierre nodded to an employee operating a lift like the ones she'd seen in the department stores in New York. The employee opened the doors to the lift, and they all stepped on, crowding inside. Clay was finally able to greet Harvey and Roger while the lift carried them up to the third floor.

Stepping off the lift, they had arrived in the elegant clubhouse. They had a view of the entire racecourse through some large windows straight ahead. Pierre paused to speak with another employee while they took in the magnificent view. Aunt Mae was huffing a little from the walk to the lift and looked as though she could use a rest.

Gladdie stepped up to the windows and gazed down at the racetrack. "Look, Clay! How fast the agents are able to place bets on their totalizer machines! They have many convenient stations set up. We'll have to mention this to Colonel Winn."

Clay nodded while she counted three stations set up in the middle of the track where the infield seating was located, two more stations where people milled in front of the stands, and another station on each end of the track. Seven machines in total?

No, for a glance over her shoulder revealed two more stations between separate dining areas there in the clubhouse. Longchamps must have at least nine or ten stations, as there might well be more hidden from her view. The Kentucky Derby wasn't quite as large as all of this yet, but she could see why they would need to find those machines in Louisville to make the day a smooth success.

Each of the operators had large chalkboards on wheels beside them to post changes to the incoming bets. The outdoor operators wore the cumbersome machines strapped to their bodies. No telling how heavy they were. A few stations placed the machines on tables, like those inside the clubhouse and in front of the stands.

The operators typed in the bets as bettors stepped up to them. Then the machines spit out slips of paper which the operators handed to each bettor. It all seemed quite organized. She didn't quite understand how the machines communicated with each other, but Colonel Winn should know more about that.

"Yes, Gladdie, you are correct. These stations are exactly the sort of thing Winn will want to know about." Clay pointed out the stations to Harvey and Roger, who lugged their equipment closer. "Harvey, can you and Roger get some photographs of those totalizer stations once Pierre leads us to our seats?"

Harvey smiled, pushing his glasses up on the bridge of his nose. "Sure thing, Clay."

"Just don't lose that bottle of bourbon." Aunt Mae wagged her finger at Clay, sassy again now that she had recovered a little of her strength. "I'm not going to run all over this city scavenging for another if you lose it. And it's quite possible that no one in Paris has a replacement for our fine Kentucky bourbon."

Clay grinned and clutched the box containing the

gift. "I'll keep an eye on it. We can hide it under our table."

Pierre was on the move again, beckoning them to follow. Uh-oh! Gladdie picked up her skirts and urged her party along with a wave. The concierge soon seated them at a spacious linen-covered table near a balcony door with an excellent view of the finish line. A centerpiece of pale pink peonies in a crystal vase made her smile. They could step out onto the balcony to observe the races or view them from the enormous wall of windows running along the wall at the end of their table.

Aunt Mae plopped into a seat and snapped open her fan with a harrumph. She waved it with vigor. "If I keel over from exhaustion, do try the smelling salts inside my purse before carrying me out on a stretcher. The salts will be more dignified."

Anyone who could wave a fan with that much velocity was not likely to pass out, but no doubt the distance they'd covered had been a strain on her dear aunt. Gladdie's feet ached from all of the walking and standing in line, and they had only just arrived.

She leaned over her aunt, touching her plump shoulder. "How about some sweet tea to revive us?"

Aunt Mae's eyes widened and she smiled, still fluttering her fan. "Please, oui!"

Pierre gestured to a waiter who stepped over to assist them, handing them menus. "I'll return after the races with Jean-Claude. We'll have those machines ready for you. I hope you all enjoy the day. Best wishes to your horse. Now, if I may introduce you to your waiter, Monsieur Frederic. He'll take good care of you."

"Call me Frederic," the man said, stepping forward.

"Merci beaucoup, Pierre. Bonjour, Frederic." Clay shook the concierge's outstretched hand, causing Gladdie to smile again as Pierre dashed away. Yet another thing to love about her fiancé. His French wasn't bad for a Kentucky boy...and he was already asking their waiter for a pitcher of sweet tea and ordering a variety of appetizers—stuffed mushroom caps, chicken salad croissants, fruit salad, and melba toast with brie. Bless the man!

"Just something to start our meal with, mind you," Clay said when the waiter scurried away. "Peruse the menus and order whatever you like. I'm going to order the *Steak au Poivre*."

"A man after my heart. Thank you for ordering something right away. Once again, I find myself famished." Aunt Mae looked down at her menu. "I'll try the Chicken Divan. They serve it in New York, too, and it's one of my favorites."

"I'll have the steak as well," Harvey said.

"Steak sounds good to me," Roger agreed. "Then we'll get to taking photographs down on the track."

Gladdie scanned the selections. "I'll try the *Poulet Chausseur*." They would be ready to order when Frederic returned to their table with those appetizers.

Now, to observe those totalizer machines in action!

And soon, Moon Lily would be the main action, turning everyone's head...

~

The time for the main race finally drew near, and Gladdie, Clay, and Aunt Mae stepped out onto the balcony. Red and Carter were standing down on the sidelines, leaning against a railing with other trainers and grooms. Harvey and Roger were busy down below, looking for the perfect angle and taking photographs. The jockeys had mounted their steeds, and Gladdie prayed for Charlie and their prized filly. "C'mon Moon Lily! You can do it," she said under her breath as the horses lined up at the starting line.

The gunshot sounded and Moon Lily took off. Clay grasped Gladdie's hand and squeezed as her mouth dropped open, for their horse took the lead from the beginning...and held it the entire way. That determined filly didn't want anyone to beat her. She finished the one-and-a-quarter-mile race nearly half a furlong ahead of the others.

Clay picked Gladdie up and twirled her around. She laughed with unbridled glee. When they arrived at the winner's circle with their crew, Clay wrapped an arm around her waist for the official photo. They'd be returning to Kentucky with two large winning purses from their whirlwind tour of Europe. And Velvet Brooks was secure.

"Are you happy?" he murmured as Gladdie reached out and patted Moon Lily for a job well done.

"Oh Clay..." She turned and smiled up into his blue eyes. "I've never been this happy in my whole life."

He grinned. "Good. *Fait accompli*, as they say. Now hold that trophy up high. Here comes Harvey with Roger...and about ten other photographers."

Harvey hollered, "Everyone smile!" Photographers snapped their photos, and Gladdie breathed a sigh of relief. At last, she could start the next phase of her life.

"What will you and Clay do after the Derby and your wedding are over?" Harvey shouted to them with his pencil poised over a notepad.

"That's easy." Gladdie grinned up at Clay. "We'll live happily ever after."

EPILOGUE

MAY 23, 1908
VELVET BROOKS

"Welcome home to Kentucky!" Colonel Winn's voice boomed over the telephone in Pa's study where Gladdie and Clay leaned close together to share the news of their arrival. "I read every article in Harvey's column documenting the journey. Congratulations to Moon Lily!"

"Thank you, Colonel Winn." Gladdie exchanged a smile with Clay.

"I thought you might be interested to know we found the other three machines. The bad news is, as we suspected, they were in poor condition. The mechanics are working on them as we speak. If they can't get them fixed, the ones you brought back from Paris will be of even greater value. Either way, we'll be able to proceed as planned, in great part due to what you and Clay have done."

Clay bent over the telephone. "Thank you, Colonel Winn. Glad we could help. Gladdie and I will deliver the machines to Churchill Downs tomorrow afternoon when we board Moon Lily for the big day."

"Excellent, excellent. See you and Moon Lily then." Colonel Winn disconnected the line.

Gladdie hung the receiver on its stand and released a happy sigh. "We did it."

"And your pa will be home in time for the Derby. I have to admit, I'm a little nervous about seeing him again after all these years." Clay's brows furrowed.

They'd only been home for a day, but she held up an envelope containing a letter from Chesapeake Manor. "Don't worry. I received a letter from Mama. She said again she and Pa are thrilled about our engagement, and she reminded me we're planning a big church wedding."

He pulled her into an embrace and kissed her. "And a big wedding you shall have."

The idea of a lavish social affair made her a little nervous, but at least they'd set a date for September, and Pa would be able to walk her down the aisle. "I still can't get over how many people turned up to welcome us home at the train station." It seemed as if the whole of Lexington had followed their journey to save the Derby, and hence their engagement, and all of Clay's kisses, through Harvey's column.

When carriage wheels rattled on the drive, Gladdie stepped back from Clay as she exchanged a curious look with him. A moment later, Martin greeted Delia and Jake as they came inside the house.

Delia bustled through the open door into the library with a huge smile on her face and Jake on her heels. "You'll never guess what the doctor just told us." She threw her arms out wide. "We're having twins!"

"What? Are you sure?" Gladdie glanced at Jake, who nodded, confirming the news.

"Yes, we've come straight from my appointment. The doctor seemed sure. He wants me to get more rest." Her sister waddled toward a chair on the other side of Pa's desk and sank into it, a hand over her growing tummy. "I can hardly believe it."

"Congratulations, Jake, Delia!" Clay reached across the desk and shook hands with Jake.

"That's wonderful news!" Gladdie came around the desk, and leaning down, she gave her sister a hug. "Ruby, Ella, Mary, and Dora will be thrilled. Have you told them yet?"

Delia's eyes wide, she shook her head and laughed. "No, not yet. We can hardly believe it ourselves. That'll make six children under our roof."

"We're hoping for boys, or maybe a boy and a girl, but we'll be glad for healthy children and whatever gender the Lord gives us. However, we only stopped by to share the news with you." Jake turned toward his wife. "Honey, it's time to get you home. You need to put your feet up or go right to bed."

"Yes, I think you're right." Delia wore a stunned expression that probably wouldn't go away for a few days at least. "May I have dinner on a tray in bed this evening?"

"You can have whatever your heart desires." Turning to her and Clay, Jake added, "I know we said it yesterday at your homecoming, but congratulations again about Moon Lily and saving the best race in Kentucky." He pulled Delia upright and sent a wink and a goodbye nod in their direction as he ushered his sweetheart toward Lottie Belle.

After the front door closed behind them, Gladdie offered Clay an apologetic smile. "I think I'll tell Grace and Willamena that I'll have dinner in bed tonight too. I'm worn out from our journey. You won't mind if I call it a night early, will you?"

He chuckled and kissed her nose. "I was thinking the same thing. I'll head to Lottie Belle for dinner, story time with Ollie and Emery, and will call it an early night as well. We need our rest so we can get Moon Lily, Red, Carter, and Charlie, *and* those machines to Churchill Downs by tomorrow afternoon."

They stepped outside onto the veranda where Clay gave her a sweet kiss before saying goodnight. It would be difficult to part with him each night until September. But how silly of her to ponder missing him when she had only three months to plan her wedding. Not to mention the work of beginning to furnish and decorate a mansion. And they would want to spend plenty of time with Ollie and Emery. With her parents and family returning in just a few days, there'd be a welcome home dinner to plan too.

No, they wouldn't have much time to miss each other. They would be so busy, three months would speed right by.

~

MAY 30, 1908

CHURCHILL DOWNS, THE KENTUCKY DERBY, LOUISVILLE

Moon Lily was already a heroine to the crowds when Gladdie arrived at the racecourse with Clay and all of her family the following Saturday. Folks even held up posters with the filly's name, and she was one of the favorites for bettors. For the first time in years, the Derby would not take place on the first Saturday in May, but at least the 1908 Derby would indeed go on.

Pa relied on his cane to navigate his way to the special clubhouse seating Colonel Winn had promised them—in a private dining room with a balcony box— but he no longer suffered from any speech impediment, and Gladdie was extra thankful Colonel Winn had made arrangements for the entire family to sit together. In fact, the colonel joined them with his family too.

Delia had made adorable matching hats for her daughters, and one for Ollie too. Ollie sat beside Gladdie, and Emery sat next to Clay, both of them wearing spring suits. The machines were stationed at all of the right places, and Colonel Winn gave them occasional updates about how well the clerks were doing at entering the bets.

Finally, it was time for the most exciting event of all, the Kentucky Derby. No other race meant so much to Gladdie or her family members. No doubt other Kentuckians and racing enthusiasts shared the sentiment. Only a few fillies had ever won the Derby before, but if any filly could, their exceptional Moon Lily could triumph in this run for the roses. When Charlie appeared astride the beautiful chestnut filly who'd performed a stunning feat at her English debut and in Paris, racing fans cheered as Gladdie had never heard them cheer before for a horse and jockey.

"I'm so excited to see Moon Lily race today, Gladdie!" Veronica, who'd brought a healthy Creighton home from South Carolina, reached across Clay to squeeze her hand and offer an encouraging smile.

Gladdie smiled in return, but the encouragement meant a lot to her. What if something went wrong and Moon Lily's fans were disappointed? Horses could be unpredictable creatures. Nor should she be too sure of her horse because of two previous wins.

A gunshot made her jump. It usually did, no matter how many times she expected it. Her skin tingled with excitement when Moon Lily left the starting gate at a great stride. Two other horses slipped ahead, but they didn't have a big lead. Moon Lily was somewhere in the middle of the pack around the first turn, then the second turn, and the third turn.

Gladdie bit her lower lip and prayed as the horses headed into the final quarter mile. Then Charlie and his jersey colors began moving up. Gladdie rose to her feet, clasping her hands together. The filly passed two more horses. Then, in her beautiful way, Moon Lily emerged from the pack, breaking away into a clear lead.

Go, go, go!

Seconds later, Moon Lily crossed the finish line in glorious fashion, with a few stallions closing in on her tail but too far behind to capture the roses. Moon Lily had just won the Kentucky Derby!

The whole family jumped to their feet, cheering. Colonel Winn was even cheering for Moon Lily, and the horse's fans seemed to go wild. Pa said they would all walk over to the winner's circle together, but this would be Gladdie's gold cup to accept.

G laddie wrote a journal entry that night.

I've learned so much about life, such as...
   No season of affliction lasts forever.
   Without Jesus, I would be lost and counted as nothing.

Forgiveness is crucial.

God's people bloom in adversity.

Everyone deserves a second chance.

Continuing on as a good soldier of Christ is essential.

Without a dream, the people perish.

Sometimes things are not as they seem.

Not all modern inventions are bad.

A truly amazing horse like Moon Lily may only come along once in a lifetime, so seize an opportunity when it presents itself.

Dreams are worth fighting for.

Love covers a multitude of sins.

Clay is truly my hero.

The sick and wounded need and deserve our compassion.

Faith can move mountains.

On the third Saturday in September, before all of their friends and family, Pa proudly walked Gladdie down the aisle. She exchanged wedding vows with Clay, becoming Mrs. Clay Grinstead. Veronica and Delia were her brides-maids, and Olympia, the flower girl. Emery filled the role of ring bearer, and Edward and Jake were the groomsmen for Clay.

Their reception took place at the Hickory Chase ballroom.

One year later, Hickory Chase School for Orphans opened, with Gladdie and Clay as the directors of the school. They enrolled their first ten students on scholarships sponsored by various members of the Lexington community.

They also spent a great deal of time with Clay's family as Gladdie became a champion for Cora. Their wedding reintroduced Cora to society, and Gladdie continued to work with her, encouraging her socially and with her endeavors in artwork. Eventually, Cora became an art teacher specializing in drawing and painting at their school.

Callie and Aurelia both met someone special at Clay and Gladdie's wedding...and suffice it to say, relationships blossomed.

Clay and Gladdie went on to have three children of their own and lived happily ever after.

The End

Dear Reader,

I hope you enjoyed *The Debutante's Second Chance*, Book 3 of *Kentucky Debutantes of the Gilded Age*. This story concludes the series, though I look forward to writing more stories about horses and Kentucky too. I loved the characters so much that it wouldn't surprise me at all if a Book 4 happened along.

In writing this fictional story, I'm thrilled to share that it is loosely based on the true story of how Colonel Matt Winn saved the 1908 Kentucky Derby. I'm not sure where they ultimately found the three machines that Clark brought back from Paris, but I hope one day I'll find out more about this part of the true story. We do know that they were found, but in disrepair, and mechanics indeed worked on them to make them ready.

Colonel Winn didn't send anyone to Paris because

they didn't have time to do so, but I thought it would be fun to take readers to Gilded Age Europe for at least a glimpse. He also didn't push the date of the Derby back as far as I did for this fictionalized account. Winn is beloved and known for romanticizing the Kentucky Derby during his tenure as the president of Churchill Downs. The actual winner of the 1908 Derby was Stone Street on a muddy track for the slowest run in Derby history. I also moved the dates for the European races around to accommodate my story.

Regret, Genuine Risk, and Winning Colors were the only female horses to win the Derby in 1915, 1980, and 1988.

Moon Lily is a fictional horse, but I hope you enjoyed getting to know her.

Most of all, I hope you enjoyed all of the books in this series. Thank you in advance for your kind reviews.

Lisa

Did you enjoy this book? We hope so!
**Would you take a quick minute to leave a review
where you purchased the book?**
It doesn't have to be long. Just a sentence or two telling
what you liked about the story!

Receive a FREE ebook and get updates when new Wild
Heart books release: https://wildheartbooks.org/
newsletter

ABOUT THE AUTHOR

Lisa M. Prysock is a *USA Today* Bestselling, Award-Winning Christian and Inspirational Author. She and her husband of more than twenty-five years reside in beautiful, rural Kentucky. They have five children, grown. Empty nesters, they are slowly reclaiming the house.

She writes in the genres of both Historical Christian Romance and Contemporary Christian Romance, including a multi-author Western Christian Romance series, "Whispers in Wyoming." She is also the author of a devotional. Lisa enjoys sharing her faith in Jesus through her writing and has authored more than 50 published books in both Contemporary and Historical Christian Romance. She loves to make readers laugh and enjoys writing humor in many of her stories.

Lisa has many interests, but a few of these include gardening, cooking, drawing, sewing, crochet, cross stitch, reading, swimming, biking, and walking. She loves dollhouses, cats, horses, butterflies, hats, boots, flip-flops, espadrilles, chocolate, coffee, tea, chocolate, the colors peach and purple, and everything old-fashioned.

She adopted the slogan of "The Old-Fashioned Everything Girl" because of her love for classic, traditional, and old-fashioned everything. When she isn't writing, she can sometimes be found teaching herself piano and violin but finds the process "a bit slow and painful." Lisa enjoys working with the children and youth in her local church creating human videos, plays, or programs incorporating her love for inspirational dance. A few of her favorite authors include Jane Austen, Lucy Maude Montgomery, Louisa May Alcott, Charlotte Brontë, and Laura Ingalls Wilder. You'll find "Food, Fashion, Faith, and Fun" in her novels. Occasionally, she includes her own illustrations.

She continues the joy and adventure of her writing journey as a member of ACFW (American Christian Fiction Writers) and LCW (Louisville Christian Writers). Lisa's books are clean and wholesome, inspirational, romantic, and family oriented. She gives a generous portion of the proceeds to missions.

Discover more about this author at **www.Lisa-Prysock.com** where you'll find the links to purchase more of her books, free recipes, devotionals, author video interviews, book trailers, giveaways, blog posts, and much more, including an invitation to sign up for her free newsletter.

Connect with Lisa:

*Lisa's Author Website:
https://www.LisaPrysock.com
*Lisa's Facebook Reader & Friends Group:
https://www.facebook.com/groups/500592113747995/
*Follow Lisa on Goodreads:
https://www.goodreads.com/author/show/7324280.Lisa_M_Prysock
*Get a Free Book When You Sign Up for Lisa's FREE Newsletter:
https://www.LisaPrysock.com/sign_up_for_my_newsletter

If you love historical romance, check out the other Wild Heart books!

A Not So Peaceful Journey by Sandra Merville Hart

Dreams of adventure send him across the country. She prefers to keep her feet firmly planted in Ohio.

Rennie Hill has no illusions about the hardships in life, which is why it's so important her beau, John Welch, keeps his secure job with the newspaper. Though he hopes to write fiction, the unsteady pay would mean an end to their plans, wouldn't it?

John Welch dreams of adventure worthy of storybooks, like Mark Twain, and when two of his short stories are published, he sees it as a sign of future success. But while he's dreaming big with his head in the clouds, his girl has her feet firmly planted, and he can't help wondering if she really believes in him.

When Rennie must escort a little girl to her parents' home in San Francisco, John is forced to alter his plans to travel across the country with them. But the journey proves far more adventurous than either of them expect.

~

Ranger to the Rescue by Renae Brumbaugh Green

Amelia Cooper has sworn off lawmen for good.

Now any man who wants to claim the hand of the intrepid reporter had better have a safe job. Like attorney Evan Covington. Amelia is thrilled when the handsome lawyer comes courting. But when the town enlists him as a Texas Ranger, Amelia isn't sure she can handle losing another man to the perils of keeping the peace.

Evan never expected his temporary appointment to sink his relationship with Amelia. Or to instantly plunge them headlong into danger. But when Amelia and his sister are both kidnapped, the newly minted lawman must rescue them—if he's to have any chance at love

A Heart's Forever Home by Lena Nelson Dooley

A single lawyer whose clients think he needs a wife.
A woman who needs a forever home...or a forever family...or a forever love.

Although Traesa Killdare is a grown woman now, the discovery that her adoption wasn't finalized sends her reeling. Especially when her beloved grandmother dies and the only siblings she's ever known exile her from the family property without a penny to her name.

Wilson Pollard works hard for the best interest of his law clients, even those who think a marriage would make him more "suitable" in his career. And when the beloved granddaughter of a recently deceased client comes to him for help, he knows he must do whatever necessary to make her situation better.

As each of their circumstances worsen, a marriage of convenience seems the only answer for both. Traesa can't help but fall for her new husband—the man who's given her both his home and his name. But what will it take for Wilson to realize he loves her? Will a not-so-natural disaster open his eyes and heart?